Carey Cove Midwives

Delivering babies around the clock at Christmastime!

It's Christmas in Carey Cove, a bustling seaside town on the stunning Cornish coastline, where a team of dedicated midwives are poised to deliver long-awaited bundles of joy, day *or* night! While decorations are going up, fairy lights are being turned on and Santa is doing the rounds, these midwives are busy doing exactly what they do best, wherever they're most needed. But could this magical festive season, with mistletoe pinned up around every corner, also be the perfect opportunity for the staff of Carey House to follow their hearts…and finally find love?

Don't be late for these special deliveries with…

Christmas with the Single Dad Doc
by Annie O'Neil

Festive Fling to Forever
by Karin Baine

Christmas Miracle on Their Doorstep
by Ann McIntosh

Single Mom's Mistletoe Kiss
by Rachel Dove

All available now!

Dear Reader,

I have a dear friend back home in Jamaica who grew up in Cornwall, and I've always been fascinated by her stories about that intriguing county. It's one of the many places on my travel bucket list, so I was thrilled to be asked to participate in the Christmas in Carey Cove continuity. By the time I was finished writing this book, I wanted to book a trip and spend my holidays there!

My couple, Nya and Theo, could never have expected their Christmas would include a beautiful baby girl being left on the doorstep of the cottage hospital. Nor could they have anticipated the changes Hope, as they call her, would cause in their lives—and in their relationship! It's the perfect Christmas miracle for two people who deserve that little extra bit of grace the season sometimes brings.

I hope you love Nya, Theo and Hope as much as I do, and that *Christmas Miracle on Their Doorstep* gives you that warm, fuzzy feeling.

May peace, joy and health be ours this year, and for many years to come.

Ann McIntosh

CHRISTMAS MIRACLE ON THEIR DOORSTEP

—

ANN McINTOSH

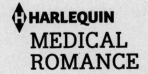

HARLEQUIN

MEDICAL
ROMANCE

Special thanks and acknowledgement are given to Ann McIntosh
for her contribution to the Carey Cove Midwives miniseries.

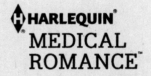

Recycling programs
for this product may
not exist in your area.

ISBN-13: 978-1-335-73750-2

Christmas Miracle on Their Doorstep

Harlequin Enterprises ULC
22 Adelaide St. West, 41st Floor
Toronto, Ontario M5H 4E3, Canada
www.Harlequin.com

Printed in U.S.A.

Ann McIntosh was born in the tropics, lived in the frozen north for a number of years, and now resides in sunny central Florida with her husband. She's a proud mama to three grown children, loves tea, crafting, animals (except reptiles!), bacon and the ocean. She believes in the power of romance to heal, inspire and provide hope in our complex world.

Books by Ann McIntosh

Harlequin Medical Romance

A Summer in São Paulo

Awakened by Her Brooding Brazilian

The Surgeon's One Night to Forever
Surgeon Prince, Cinderella Bride
The Nurse's Christmas Temptation
Best Friend to Doctor Right
Christmas with Her Lost-and-Found Lover
Night Shifts with the Miami Doc
Island Fling with the Surgeon
Christmas Miracle in Jamaica
How to Heal the Surgeon's Heart
One Night Fling in Positano

Visit the Author Profile page at Harlequin.com.

For Mary-Eve, who loves Christmas romances best.
Thank you for your friendship and support!

CHAPTER ONE

Nya Ademi took off her seldom-used reading glasses and blinked rapidly. Normally she didn't have to put them on immediately on arriving at work but waited until the afternoon, after a day particularly heavy with paperwork. But this morning she'd woken up with scratchy eyes and gummy lashes, as though she'd been crying during the night. Unable to go back to sleep, she'd come into work at a ridiculously early hour.

She couldn't remember her dreams but it was possible, of course, that she'd shed a few tears. After all, the day before had been an emotional one, although she wouldn't classify it as sad, really. There had been times when she'd even laughed.

Like when the wind had pushed her along the pavement, and she'd clutched the shiny balloons by their strings so they wouldn't blow away in the blustery autumn weather.

She'd been using her body to shield the flowers in her other hand, worried all the petals would be blown off if she didn't protect them. It would have been ridiculous to arrive with just a bunch of stems, rather than the bouquet of lovely red roses.

The thought of it happening had made Nya snort, knowing Jim would find such an eventuality infinitely amusing. She could so easily picture him doubled over, his deep barks of laughter echoing through the air.

'Just stems,' she'd imagined him wheezing, tears gathering in his gorgeous brown eyes and laugh lines turning his face into a landscape of mirth. 'Not one flower left, after that heap of dosh you spent on them.'

She'd giggled, then, and had still been chuckling to herself as she'd turned into the cemetery then made her way to his grave.

Now, pinching the bridge of her nose, she allowed a sensation of unreality to wash over her.

Jim's fiftieth birthday.

His being gone for almost twenty years.

Although Jim was always in her heart, most days she was fine—going on with her life with a smile—but even now waves of grief and loss could bowl her over. No longer as fresh as they once were, but heartbreaking just the same.

Yesterday, however, had been planned and she'd expected to feel far worse than she actually had. She never went to Jim's grave on Remembrance Day. On November eleventh she went to the cenotaph here in Carey Cove to pay her respects to all the men and women who'd served. Jim's day was always December first.

His birthday.

And enough time had passed that she didn't need to go every year, so now she kept her trips to Andover to milestones. His fortieth, and forty-fifth. Yesterday, his fiftieth.

During her time there, alone beside his grave, she thought about him in a way she didn't allow herself to the rest of the time.

Remembering his smile, his laughter and tenderness. The way he'd cared so deeply about her and his family. About the plans they'd made, oh, so long ago now. Sometimes she'd even allow herself to slip into a fantasy where he hadn't been killed in combat, and those plans had miraculously come to fruition.

Perhaps it wasn't surprising, then, that while she hadn't really felt sad yesterday, the agony of loss had crept up on her last night, while she slept.

Pushing her glasses up on her nose, she determinedly forced her attention back to the schedule she'd been working on. As Head Midwife of the Carey Cove cottage hospital, she had to evenly distribute the workload, which just now took some fancy footwork. She had a newish midwife—Kiara—who was working out well, and a trainee—Lorna— who needed her supervision. With another midwife—Marnie—out on maternity leave, and her replacement delayed for another two weeks, Nya had to juggle to keep the midwifery centre and maternity ward running efficiently.

When someone knocked on her office door, it was almost a relief to be interrupted, but she was surprised when her mother, rather than one of her co-workers, came in.

It was at moments like this, when she saw her mother unexpectedly, that she realised why one of her friends from nursing school had compared Mum to an *orisa*. With her wonderfully straight-backed posture and dark skin beautifully set off by her intricate green, gold, and red headwrap—a *gele* today—she looked the epitome of an African goddess.

While Nya had inherited her mother's

smooth complexion and plump, curvy figure, she knew she didn't have the older lady's regal bearing.

'Mum. What are you doing here so early?' she asked, glancing at her watch as she went around her desk to kiss her mother's cheek. 'It's just gone six.'

'I was on my way to Penzance for the textile seminar but wanted to see you,' her mother replied, in her usual crisp tones. 'I stopped by your cottage and realised you weren't home, so came here. You really should lock the front door when you're here alone this early.'

Nya wrinkled her nose.

'This is Carey Cove, Mum. Not exactly a dangerous place.'

Iona's raised eyebrows spoke volumes, but she didn't pursue the discussion. Instead she said, 'I wanted to show you this.'

She'd been unbuttoning her hunter-green coat as she spoke and, when she opened it, Nya gasped, then clapped as she saw her mother's sweater.

'You got it finished,' she exclaimed. 'It's lovely!'

Mum smiled, glancing down at the garment in question. 'Just in time, too.'

Iona had been working on a new knitting

pattern, using two African fabrics—*aso oke* and *kente*—as the inspiration. Nya knew just how much work she'd put into trying to get it finished in time for the special presentation at the university, given by a visiting expert on African textiles and weaving.

'Now I want one,' she said.

Mum laughed and shook her head. 'You know how bad I am at writing patterns, but if you want to look at my notes and try for yourself…'

Nya couldn't help giggling at the thought. Mum's handwriting—normally perfectly legible—somehow turned to chicken-scratch when she was designing a new knitting pattern, and that fact was a longstanding joke between them.

'I'd need an interpreter to do that,' Nya replied, still laughing.

Mum clicked her tongue, as though in disapproval, but was still smiling as she sat down in the visitor's chair. Then her smile faded and Nya was the recipient of a sharp, penetrating look, along with a nod of her head towards Nya's chair on the other side of the desk. It reminded her why Iona Bradford's university students had been terrified of their professor of English literature and

African studies. Retirement hadn't softened that steely look.

Taking the less than subtle hint, Nya went back around to her own chair and sat down, wondering what to expect. One never knew with Mum.

Raising a hand to touch her *gele*, Mum asked, 'How did yesterday go?'

Nya hadn't said she was going to the cemetery, but wasn't surprised that Mum guessed where she'd been. What did surprise her was that her mother had brought it up. For the last five years, ever since they'd argued about Nya's apparently unwillingness to get involved in another relationship, they'd avoided talking about Jim.

'I don't mind if you've decided not to have children, even though I feel you'd make a marvellous mother,' Mum had said back then. 'But you've locked yourself—your heart— away, and it's not healthy.'

That Mum had spoken about Jim, and Nya's trip to the cemetery, now felt a little like a minefield.

'It was good. Even had a bit of a giggle.'

As Nya told her mother about the flowers, and what she thought Jim would have said, her mother nodded.

'I can imagine his reaction too,' she replied, a small smile pulling at the corner of her lips. 'He did have an amazing, if quirky, sense of humour. Such a zest for life. I don't think he was afraid of anything.' She hesitated, as though about to say something more, then glanced at her watch. 'Well, I must get going or I'll be late for the seminar.'

Nya rounded the desk again to receive her mother's goodbye kiss, and another of those penetrating looks. 'I've been invited by the bursar to stay on after the seminar and have dinner with the faculty and Dr Agyapong, but I can come back instead and meet you at The Dolphin, if you like.'

Nya gave her mother another hug, and said, 'Of course not, Mum. I'm behind on my paperwork here, so it's probably best I stay late this evening and get it done. We'll have our usual dinner next week.'

Not exactly true, about the paperwork, since although she had been behind, she was almost completely caught up now. But her mother's visit, and the fact she'd asked about the trip to the cemetery, had Nya on high alert, sensing there was something more Mum wanted to say, but hadn't. It was probably better to let a few days go by before they had that talk, whatever it entailed.

The last thing Nya wanted was to argue with Mum again.

Hopefully, by the time her mother came back to Carey Cove, she'd turn her mind to Christmas, and the small mountain of half-finished gifts still in her yarn bag. Iona kept a small bedsit in Penzance, as well as a cottage in Carey Cove, splitting her time between the two. Often once she got to Penzance and started socialising with friends and old co-workers, she ended up staying a few days.

After walking her mother out to the vestibule and going back into her office, Nya couldn't help thinking back on the conversation—and the long-ago argument too.

She'd never been able to understand Mum's attitude.

It was as though she'd completely forgotten the fact she never remarried after Nya's father died. Why, then, was it so difficult to understand her daughter's choices? They'd both mourned, long and hard, and turned to their professions as a source of solace and meaning.

Nya hadn't had the chance to have the babies Jim and she had talked about, but helping other women bring healthy children into the world gave her the greatest satisfaction.

Besides, she thought as she pulled her chair

closer to her desk again, even if she were interested in a relationship, it wasn't as though Carey Cove was overrun with eligible men. And she hadn't come back here in the hopes of finding love in her childhood village—just peace and a modicum of happiness.

She'd achieved that, and more, she reminded herself stoutly, pulling the schedule closer.

And she was absolutely content.

Dr Theo Turner drove through the still-quiet streets of Carey Cove, trying to jolly himself out of his sour mood. The world seemed intent on making him miserable just now, and although the last year and a half had been extremely difficult, he refused to allow unhappiness to become habitual.

Hard not to, though, when everything felt so incredibly unsettled and he was trying—and failing—to adapt to a new normal.

One where he lived the life of a divorced man, battling loneliness by working as hard as possible, and even considered leaving Carey Cove—a place he loved, but no longer felt he belonged.

A light mist lay over the picturesque village, giving the landscape a ghostly air. As he approached the main road, he saw a car go past towards Penzance, and recognised Iona Bradford by her colourful headscarf, but was too far away to wave. Once he got to the centre of the village, he glimpsed Avis Mitchell on the green, training one of her German shepherds.

She glanced up as he passed, but didn't acknowledge him.

Colin Duncan was making his way towards his small shop and post office. The older man waved and smiled, and Theo lifted a hand in return, yet found himself wondering if Colin's greeting came from friendliness, or just familiarity.

Strange to have such thoughts when he'd lived in Carey Cove for twenty years—had felt completely comfortable up until Femi, in the midst of an argument, had accused him of being a visitor in his own home.

'You come and go as you please. Spend more time in Falmouth with your patients than at home with your wife and children. TJ and Gillian hardly know you, much less the people here in Carey Cove. You might as well set up house in the blasted hospital. You probably enjoy being with your co-workers best anyway.'

Highly unfair, he'd thought at the time, and still did. Yes, his profession made a lot of demands on his time. Mothers and babies didn't adhere to schedules when they went into distress—a fact he'd explained to his children as soon as he thought they were old enough to understand.

Femi had taken exception to that too, accusing him of trying to avoid his responsibilities by sloughing all the daily graft off on her, and getting the children onboard with it. Pointing out it had been her decision to give up her clinical psychology practice and become a stay-at-home mum hadn't gained him any brownie points. And his suggestion that she hire help so it didn't all fall on her only caused another row.

But he'd been determined to give his children everything he hadn't had as a child.

Stability.

A father who was a responsible member of society and could provide them with whatever they needed.

And he'd also done his best to be there for them as much as possible. They'd had uninterrupted days out, family holidays, and he'd spent umpteen hours on the touchline of rugby games, at piano recitals, and all their other activities. Intellectually he knew, despite what Femi intimated, that his relationship with his children was solid, but the seeds of doubt she'd planted had flourished.

He now felt a stranger in his own life.

Usually by now, at the beginning of December, he'd be getting excited about Christmas. Planning surprises for his children, even though they were both grown—Gillian already out of university and working in London, TJ in his second to last year at Cambridge. Thinking about getting a tree, and taking dedicated time off to decorate it and the cottage.

Femi had put paid to any enthusiasm he might have had, by the expedient method of shutting him out of the holiday festivities with his children.

'Devi and I are having a big family get-together,' she'd said on the phone last night. 'I've already told the children that they're expected on the twenty-third, and that they're to stay as long as they like. Gillian said she's due back at work on the twenty-seventh, but TJ will stay until it's time to go back to uni.'

Theo's heart had sunk, and he'd been trying to find the right way to express his disappointment when Femi had continued, in the acidic tone he knew all too well.

'Please don't harass the children about coming to see you. It will just upset them.

Besides, I'm sure you're glad, since that lets you spend as much time as you want at St Isolde's and you don't have to think about anything but yourself and your patients.'

He hadn't told her that the powers-that-be had forced him to take time off, since he'd been working non-stop for the last eighteen months. Femi was, in his opinion, having more than enough fun at his expense.

And he hated feeling so bitter about it all.

Even the sight of the holiday decorations all along the streets and in shop windows did nothing to buoy his spirits. In fact, they seemed to mock his dreariness and make it worse.

At least he had his office at Carey House, where he could go and hide out and, unless he told them he was there, no one would notice. After all, only if there was a patient on site would anyone be at the cottage hospital this early, and he didn't plan to go near the maternity ward. Staying alone in the house one more day could potentially drive him insane. On his office computer were at least six months' worth of medical journals and studies he wanted to read but hadn't had time to get to. They would keep his brain busy, hopefully stopping these depressing thoughts from bombarding him all day.

Once on the hospital grounds, he drove around to the side of the building and parked before climbing out and retrieving his brief-case from the rear seat.

Still deep in thought, he approached the front door, keys in hand, ready to let himself in, when he spied something on the doorstep and hesitated for a moment.

It looked like a long package of some kind, covered with a blanket, and as he strode closer his heart rate picked up. As soon as he got to the door, he put his briefcase down on the stone step, and bent to lift the edge of the blanket.

From the basket beneath, a pair of unfo-cused blue eyes blinked up at him, as though trying to figure out who he was. And then, almost in slow motion, the baby's little face grew wrinkled as he or she began to cry.

CHAPTER TWO

I⊤ WAS STILL too early for Hazel to be in to take up her post at Reception, so when Nya heard the front door of the hospital rattle, she got up to see who it was. While it wasn't unusual for them to have an expectant mother come in at all hours in labour, the midwife on call for that night would usually already have been alerted to attend. As far as she knew, that hadn't happened.

And was that the cry of a baby echoing down the corridor?

Not knowing what to think, Nya increased her pace, turning the corner into the reception area and stopping short at the sight of Theo Turner seemingly struggling to close the door behind himself.

Not surprising, since he had a basket, his briefcase and keys in hand—and a swaddled, crying baby in the crook of one arm.

The incongruity of it kept her frozen in

place for a moment. Long enough for the obstetrician to turn to face her, and when their eyes met her heart did a funny little stutter, causing a rush of heat to her face.

She'd always thought Theo was handsome. He had the type of understated good looks that caused most women to give him at least a second look, and a quiet charm that nonetheless lit up whatever room he was in.

But since they'd met, on her return to Carey Cove, he'd always been Theo, Femi's husband, an intrinsic part of a couple she knew well, so completely out of bounds in every way. To suddenly find herself aware—as if for the first time—of his good looks, and self-conscious in his presence, was shocking.

Then there was no time to wonder about her strange reaction to her old friend, as she rushed forward to relieve him of the basket and briefcase.

'Theo, what on earth…?' she asked, as she put the items down on Hazel's desk, and then instinctively reached for the baby, holding and shushing while Theo took off his coat. The slight weight in her arms, the scrunched little face, fat tears running down pinkened cheeks, all tugged at her heart.

'The baby was on the doorstep,' he replied. Before Nya knew what he intended, he'd plucked the infant from her arms and was heading towards one of the examination rooms, leaving Nya to trot to be able to keep up with his long strides. 'I don't know how long he or she's been out there.'

'Couldn't be more than ten minutes or so,' she told him, turning on the light over the examination table where he'd laid the baby, who was now wailing lustily. 'My mum left about fifteen minutes ago, and I let her out the front. Believe me, neither of us would have ignored a basket on the doorstep.'

The quick smile Theo sent her lit up his oft solemn face and caused a little fan of laugh lines to appear at the corner of each eye. Fighting another wave of heat rushing to her face, Nya looked down at the baby so as not to stare at his lips. But then she found herself watching his hands as he un-swaddled the squirming infant, and this time her own hands tingled, and the warmth spread through her belly.

'I glimpsed Iona when I was driving here, and I have no doubt what you say is true,' he replied, amusement still lingering in his voice even as it dropped to a low croon. 'There's no way super-midwife Nya wouldn't have seen you, is there, sweetheart?'

Obviously he was talking to the baby, but Nya couldn't help the little hitch of her breath.

What on earth was happening to her?

Taking herself in hand, Nya turned her thoughts to the practicality of the situation, just as Theo got the blanket undone, revealing the warm pink pyjamas beneath.

'Unless your mama is one of those people who don't go by tradition, I'm guessing you're a little girl,' he continued, in that same low, sing-song voice she'd heard him use with babies before. 'And you're in need of a clean nappy.'

Thankful for something to do, Nya rushed to the supply cupboard and retrieved a clean nappy, along with a blanket and baby wipes.

'How is her babygrow?' she asked, poised to dash off to find one to fit.

'Still dry,' Theo replied, as he took the wipe she offered him and efficiently cleaned up the little girl's bum. 'She looks to be about a week old—don't you, sweetheart? Do you recognise her?'

'No.' Nya shook her head, running a finger over the little clenched fist closest to her, and then over the wisps of light brown hair on the baby's pate. 'I'm sure she wasn't born here. I'll start a file on her, if you'll take weight and measurements, and then call Social Services.'

'She seems to be in good health,' Theo sing-songed as he replaced the pyjamas, adroitly managing to do it with a minimum of fuss. 'And Mama wrapped you up nice and warmly, so there's no hint of hypothermia.'

'I wonder what her poor mum is going through,' Nya murmured. 'She must have thought this her only option.'

'Yes,' Theo said as he gently lifted the now gurgling baby onto his shoulder. 'And brought her to a place where she knew her little one would be safe and well taken care of.'

How like him not to judge the baby's mother, Nya thought as she assembled the appropriate forms and went over to the weighing station, where Theo waited. He probably felt the way she did, that everyone deserved the benefit of the doubt. With some of the horror stories they'd heard and seen, the mother probably had done the very best she could by bringing the baby to their doorstep.

'Oh,' she said, staring down at the clipboard in her hand. 'What should we call her? I refuse to put "Baby Jane Smith" on this form.'

'Well, I should hope not,' Theo replied, amusement once more vibrating in his voice. 'She's too beautiful for a name like that.'

'That's it,' Nya said, unable to stop a little

giggle of glee from breaking through. 'How about Hope? As her name, I mean?'

'Perfect,' he replied. 'Especially at this time of year.'

And Nya couldn't help her little thrill of satisfaction at his agreement.

As they worked together examining Hope, Theo relayed the information he gathered to Nya in the same sweet croon as before, and Nya had to force herself to concentrate. Although they'd worked together in the past, and she'd heard him speak to babies this way before, for some reason today she found it unreasonably adorable.

There was something about a man with hands as large as Theo's so tenderly handling a week-or-so-old baby that just made Nya's heart melt too.

She shook her head, bringing herself up short. Maybe this was an after-effect of her mother's visit, or just her own thoughts earlier, but this was no time to let her mind wander this way.

'If you can manage by yourself for a while, I'll run down to my office and call Caroline at Social Services. We need to get Hope a safe place to stay until they can find her mum.'

Theo sent her a glance that had her heart

racing and stumbling over itself. Then he turned that dark, twinkling gaze back to the baby, who was once more safely ensconced in his arms.

'Of course we can manage. I think I'm quite qualified to take care of Hope for however long it takes.'

'Brilliant,' Nya said, tearing herself away from his and Hope's side with more difficulty than she liked, and heading out of the door. Then a thought struck her, and she turned back to ask, 'What are you doing here, anyway? I heard you were on holiday.'

The slight smile on his face faded, and his eyes grew guarded as he looked back up at her to give a negligible shrug of one shoulder. 'I thought I was coming in to do some paperwork, but it turns out I was really here to rescue this little darling—wasn't I, Hope?'

And since his somewhat dismissive tone came through clearly despite that special baby voice, Nya turned away without another word.

But it stung, all the same. They'd been friends for years, but she knew Theo had been avoiding her since his divorce and she couldn't help wondering why he'd turned so cool. Surely he didn't think she'd hit on him, as she'd heard some of the other women in the village had? Or perhaps it was the fact that she and Femi, while not good friends, had been more than acquaintances—going to lunch on occasion, or out to the pub of an evening.

She'd thought it best to give Theo space, hoping that in time he'd realise she was, if not on his side, particularly, then still a friend, but it seemed he wanted nothing to do with her, at all.

And if that was what Theo wanted, then that was what he'd get. As soon as they got Hope appropriately situated, Nya would make sure to keep her distance.

Probably for the best, with these strange emotions he'd stirred in her today!

Theo watched Nya walk away and found himself watching the sway of her hips with far more interest than he should. Somehow, this morning, he'd been aware of her in a new, disquieting way.

The gleam in her warm brown eyes.

Her gentleness as she touched baby Hope, and swept her narrow, lovely fingers over the baby's hair.

The fresh scent rising from her hair as she leant close to him, and the smooth, dark curve of her cheek, seen in three-quarter profile as she smiled.

All of those, plus that infectious giggle she always seemed to try to suppress, had filled him with the kind of joy he'd begun to think he might never feel again.

Then he'd thrown back up all the barriers she'd so easily slipped behind.

At some point he'd have to apologise. It had become instinctive, this need to keep a new distance between himself and other people. Much easier than trying to gauge who was still a friend, and who was looking askance. Realising the village grapevine had been hard at work, and people were probably talking about how he'd been forcibly sent on holiday, had caused him to treat her coolly.

Yet, he knew he was being unfair to Nya, who was the nicest, most caring person he knew. He'd often wondered how it was some lucky man hadn't snatched her up long ago, even knowing perhaps it would be impossible for any man to have a chance to do so. Everyone knew she was still in love with her husband, although it must be close to twenty years since he'd died.

Theo believed in everlasting love, so thought he understood her hesitance.

It was a shame though. Nya had so much to give and would have been a phenomenal mother.

And, he realised, he was thinking about all this so as to be able to ignore the fact that he'd hurt her feelings.

'I was a heel, wasn't I, Hope?' he asked the little girl, who was staring up at him and sucking on one hand. 'We should go find Auntie Nya, and apologise, shouldn't we? Or I should, at any rate.'

But he found himself reluctant to go after Nya. She'd so easily stirred something deep within. The kind of longing he had no business feeling.

He'd always considered her a friend, and to even for a moment wonder what it would be like to touch her, maybe even kiss her, threw him into confusion.

However, they had to work together just now, to make sure Hope got the care she needed, and, after a deep breath and a quick kiss on Hope's forearm, he made his way to Nya's office.

She was still on the phone, glancing up quickly at him as he came in her door and gesturing to the chair on the other side of her desk with her chin.

'Certainly,' she said into the receiver. 'Of course we can. Keep me informed. Thank you.'

Putting down the receiver with her habitual brisk movements, she took off her square, black-framed glasses and rubbed the side of her index finger across one eye.

'Caroline says they're run off their feet at the moment, but she'll start trying to find Hope a foster family. She'll also advise the police about you finding her, and they'll probably be by later to take our statements. In the meantime, she's asked if we can take care of Hope here.'

Hope made a little sound, and Theo looked down. The infant had fallen asleep, her fist still in her mouth, and the sweet innocence of her tugged hard at Theo's heart.

'Well,' he said, without thinking it through. 'Since I don't have anything planned for the day, why don't I take care of her until Caroline finds a suitable placement?'

Nya's face lit up, and her lush lips curled into one of her warm smiles.

'That would be brilliant,' she said, leaning back in her chair and swinging it from side to side slightly. 'I know the midwives coming on duty shortly would be willing to keep an eye on her, but unfortunately we're a bit short-staffed, and there are no patients in the maternity ward right now. If you're willing to keep an eye on her, when she's awake you can give her the physical contact she needs.'

Hope stirred against his chest, and Theo glanced down at her again, shifting her to a more comfortable position. The infant sighed, and snuggled in closer, and he couldn't help smiling down at her.

When he raised his gaze to Nya, there was a look in her eyes that froze him in place, and had his heart pounding.

Then she turned away, as though looking out of the door, and said, 'That'll be Hazel coming in. Let's go tell her what's going on, so she doesn't have a conniption when the bobbies turn up at the door.'

Before he could even move, she was out of her seat—heading for the corridor—and it took him a moment to regain his equilibrium and follow her to Reception.

CHAPTER THREE

It seemed as though every midwife, doctor, and even a few patients wanted to see Hope for themselves, and it took for ever for Nya to get Theo and the baby comfortably ensconced in his office.

'What a darling,' Sophie French cooed. 'Wait until I tell Roman about this. He'll be gobsmacked.'

'I heard best wishes are in order? Have you and Roman set a date?' Theo smiled at the midwife, who turned a beguiling shade of pink in the cheeks.

'It's all so new, we haven't got to that stage yet. You'll come to the engagement party on Christmas Eve, won't you?'

Nya saw the change in Theo. Although he was still smiling, his eyes looked sad, and she thought he seemed to retreat a little.

'I'm not sure where I'll be,' he replied. 'But if I'm here, I'll certainly come.'

And that seemed to satisfy Sophie.

When Nya suggested Theo put Hope down for her nap in the small nursery attached to the maternity ward, he immediately nixed that idea.

'We'll both be more comfortable in my office,' he said, his gaze pinned to Hope, who was still sleeping soundly in his arms. 'I'm just along from the staff room, so when she wakes up and is hungry, I don't have far to go to get her bottle.'

'If you need a break, just call down and let me know,' she told him, once they'd arranged a crib, and everything else he needed, to hand. She'd decided that, until she got these strange impulses she was experiencing around him under control, it was best to give him a wide berth.

But even so, it was hard to walk away, and she found herself stopping at the door for one last look.

Theo seemed almost mesmerised by the baby in his arms—still standing beside the crib, holding her, looking down with the tenderest expression on his face. Nya's heart seemed to expand as it raced, sending a warm, intimate sensation out into her bloodstream, until she thought she'd simply melt away.

Then, as Theo gently set Hope down in the

crib, Nya slipped out of the room, before he could notice her still watching him.

But she had to stop and take a deep breath, blinking against the moisture in her eyes, before she could go back to work.

And even though she'd decided to make herself scarce until after Social Services had collected Hope, she found herself drawn back to Theo's office over and over during the day.

Making sure both of them had everything they needed.

Taking Theo lunch when he insisted he didn't need anyone to take over Hope's care so he could go and get some.

Popping in and demanding a turn at feeding Hope when she found him just sitting down to give her a bottle.

'I'm beginning to think you don't trust me to take care of her,' Theo said, as he reluctantly relinquished the infant to Nya.

'Of course I trust you,' she replied, settling on the comfortable chair he had for visitors. 'But why should you have all the fun while I'm slogging away at work?'

That earned her a huff of laughter, and a warm glance that made her turn her gaze swiftly back to the baby in her arms.

When he looked at her like that, she wanted to shiver in reaction. Not a *bad* shiver, but the kind that had her thinking thoughts that weren't only untoward, but also wouldn't lead anywhere.

Hope twisted her head, losing the nipple for a moment, and let out a little squeak of dismay. Nya angled the bottle into place again. 'There you go, sweetheart. It's right here.'

She'd cared for hundreds, if not thousands, of babies during her time as a midwife, but there was something extra special about Hope. Perhaps it was the knowledge that the little mite was—to all intents and purposes—alone in the world that touched Nya and created the ache in her heart.

So focused was she on the baby that when Theo spoke, it was a little startling.

'I owe you an apology,' he said, in a tone that sounded both reluctant and a little defensive, as though he wasn't sure of the advisability of having the conversation.

After a swift look at his unsmiling face, Nya kept her attention on Hope, who was still happily sucking on her bottle.

'I can't think of why,' she replied, keeping her voice level with effort, as her heart did a silly double-time thump.

'I was short with you earlier—when you mentioned my being on holiday. I just…'

When his voice faded, she risked another glance his way, but found his gaze fixed on the baby in her arms, rather than on her.

'You just, what?' she asked softly, aching to see him so solemn and sad.

'I was angry when they put me on leave, and when you mentioned it, I realised that word must have got around, and that anger came back.' His lids lifted, and Nya could see the pain and uncertainty reflected in his eyes.

'We were told that you wouldn't be on call until the new year, Theo, so that's how I knew. I thought perhaps you were taking a much-deserved break and were heading off for somewhere warm and fun for a week or so.' She risked a little giggle. 'I was a bit jealous.'

One side of his mouth twisted up in an abbreviated smile that immediately faded again. 'No, I wasn't given a choice.'

She'd known him long enough to know that couldn't have sat well. But she'd also watched him overworking himself since the divorce.

'Just as well,' she rebutted mildly. 'If you had been given a choice, you wouldn't have taken it, and it's been ages since you've had any time off. Sometimes other people actually do know what's best for you.'

He got up abruptly, and walked over to the window, staring out, one hand raised to brace against the frame.

How had she never really noticed how long and strong his fingers were, until today? He really had lovely hands.

'I suppose you're right,' he said, but it didn't sound as though he were really agreeing, rather just saying what he thought she wanted to hear. 'But I don't like being forced.'

'Of course not,' she replied briskly. 'But we've all watched you working yourself into the ground, or at least seeming to. But you've been through a lot over the last eighteen months. Perhaps it's time to take a break and take stock—figure out what's best for you. Think of it in that light, and maybe it won't sting as much.'

Theo nodded, his gaze still trained out of the window, and Nya saw his chest rise on a deep breath and then, after a beat, fall again. When he turned and paced back to his chair, his expression caused a cold spot to bloom in her chest.

'That's something I've been doing, almost obsessively over the last few months,' he admitted, his deep voice almost distant, as though he was talking more to himself than to her. 'And some days I feel as though I don't belong here any more.'

The cold spot spread so rapidly Nya shivered from the onslaught of ice through her veins. And there was nothing calm or gentle about her tone when she snapped, 'What kind of nonsense talk is that?'

Hope stirred, and Nya looked down in time to see her tongue the nipple from her mouth. As the bottle was almost empty anyway, Nya shifted the infant onto her shoulder and began to rub her back.

Meeting Theo's gaze across the desk, she fixed him with the stern glare she gave recalcitrant husbands or nosy mothers-in-law, and said, 'Explain to me what on earth you're talking about.'

The look he gave her was rueful, but solemn.

'Ever since the divorce, I've felt as though my life no longer fits. That I don't really belong here in Carey Cove any more.' His lips firmed into a line, and then he shook his head. 'Femi always said I was hardly here anyway, and rattling around the cottage by myself... I just don't know where I need or want to be at the moment.'

Now *that* she understood, and she nodded,

sadness replacing whatever that cold wash of emotion had been.

'When Jim died, I couldn't stay in Andover because the memories were too hard to bear. So, I came back here, because this was where I felt safe and at home.' Unsure of whether she was expressing herself as well as she wanted to, she shook her head. 'What I mean to say is, divorce is hard, and you're entitled to grieve for as long as you want, or need to. And if getting over it—or on with a happier life—means starting afresh, I can certainly understand that impulse. But to say you don't know if you belong here? I think that's a step too far.'

Theo leaned back in his chair, his eyes fixed to her face as he said, 'Why do you think so?'

'You're an integral part of our community, and not just because you're a respected doctor. You've lived here for twenty years, and there isn't one person who hasn't turned to you—relied on you—at some point or another. I've never heard a bad word said about you by anyone. Not even Mrs. Prentiss, and you know she dislikes almost everyone.'

That brought a touch of a smile to his lips, and Nya felt her shoulders relax.

'I try to stay on Gwenda Prentiss's good

side, because she scares me,' he said dryly. Then he shrugged. 'Truthfully, this has always felt like home to me, from the first time I came to Carey House on a consult. I went back to Falmouth and told Femi I'd found where I'd like to live, and once she saw the village, she agreed it would be the ideal place to raise the children. Unfortunately, her love affair with Carey Cove didn't last. She found village life boring.' Again, a little hesitation, before he added, 'Found me and the life we were living boring.'

Deep and dangerous waters here, Nya thought, glad of the interruption when Hope let out a burp almost too big for her little body, which made both adults laugh.

'Not very ladylike, Miss Hope,' Nya said, but her mind was racing with how to respond to what Theo had said.

There was always the option to simply ignore it—change the subject to something less inflammatory—but that wasn't what a friend would do. But, despite them being divorced, was it wise to say anything that could be construed as critical of Femi?

How would that even be helpful?

Yet, Theo looked so solemn and hurt, there was no way she couldn't say what she thought. He was her friend and needed her support.

And maybe even a little of the clarity someone outside the situation could bring.

'I think,' she said slowly, then paused, searching for the right words. 'I think you need to look forward rather than back, and recognise that we're all responsible for our own happiness.'

There, that was fairly neutral, wasn't it? But Theo's eyes sharpened.

'Why do you say that?'

Trust Theo not to want to leave well enough alone, and want clarification.

Once more Nya was left picking her words carefully.

'I just think that sometimes we have to take a good look at where we are in life, and what it is we want, then make it happen. It's not up to anyone else to make us happy, you know?'

Theo opened his mouth, as though about to ask her for more details, but thankfully just then the telephone rang, and he answered. From his side of the conversation, she realised the police had arrived to take their statements, and there was no more time for the discussion.

There was no way she'd tell him that, in her opinion, Femi had made no effort to integrate into village life, and if she'd been bored and unhappy, it was mostly her own fault. The other woman had had a stable marriage, two lovely children, and the ability to do almost anything she'd wanted to make her life more fulfilled. But instead of taking whatever steps necessary, she'd chosen to blame her husband for her discontent.

Years before, when the children had got older and more independent, Femi had once more complained about boredom, and about giving up her career in psychology.

'Why don't you set up a part-time consultancy at Carey House?' Nya had suggested. 'When we need to refer patients for counselling, we have to send them to Penzance or Falmouth. It would be wonderful to have someone on hand here instead.'

They often had mothers—both expectant and postpartum—who needed professional help to work through their issues, sometimes quite urgently too.

Femi had shrugged and frowned, half-heartedly saying, 'Yeah, sure, I'll consider it, but I always want to be on hand, in case one of the children needs me.'

Nya had been forced to bite her tongue at that. Oh, she completely understood that being a stay-at-home mum was a full-time job, but Femi seemed to have forgotten how often she took off to London to shop and visit. It showed she had lots of time to herself, to do whatever she wanted.

And, of course, nothing came of Nya's suggestion.

No. Femi had seemed determined to be unhappy in Carey Cove, and perhaps in her marriage, which made it difficult for Nya to be as sympathetic towards the other woman as she would have liked.

Especially now, when it was apparent how badly Theo had been affected by the end of his marriage, to the point where he was considering leaving Carey Cove.

Just the thought made Nya in turns angry and sad, but if that was what he needed to get over Femi and move on with his life, then all she could do was be sympathetic.

Even if what she wanted was to force him to stay, although just how that would be achieved, she had no idea.

And why that was so important to her own happiness was unfathomable.

CHAPTER FOUR

AFTER NYA GAVE her statement to the constable who attended to take the report, she went back to work, leaving Theo to finish up. Once the constable departed, Theo checked on Hope, making sure she was still sleeping, then walked over to look out of his office window.

The view out over the small side garden of Carey House and down to the harbour beyond was one of his favourites and he found himself appreciating it even more than usual.

After talking with Nya, he felt a little lighter, a bit better about life.

He'd been avoiding her since the end of his marriage, and he wondered why.

He should have known she wouldn't blame him, or treat him any differently, and he now admitted how he'd allowed his guilt and doubts about himself to cloud his decisions.

It was a relief to suddenly feel less weighed

down by circumstances—a little more optimistic about the future.

Hope made a sound in her sleep, and he found himself looking over his shoulder at her, and smiling.

Having her to tend to had also helped to elevate his mood. He'd helped to birth and handled so many babies, including his own children, but that sense of falling in love with each infant never waned. It was their total innocence, and the knowledge that here was a new life just beginning, that always touched his heart.

Watching Nya feed her had filled him with warmth. It was obvious she felt the same way about Hope that he did—that although they were in the infant's life for just a short time, they would do whatever necessary to protect and nurture her.

Hopefully the police would find her mother or father quickly, and the reunion would be a safe and successful one. No one deserved to feel alone and abandoned.

Those kinds of scars were difficult to heal.

Why that made him think of Nya, he didn't want to contemplate, so he went back to his desk and pulled up the next journal he wanted to read. With one more quick glance at the sleeping baby, he turned his attention to his computer screen, and lost himself in a study about the effect of influenza during pregnancy.

When a soft knock came on his door, and Hope stirred, Theo was surprised to realise the afternoon was almost gone. He wasn't terribly surprised to see Nya come in, but there was an air of suppressed excitement about her that had him looking at her closely as he picked Hope up.

'I heard from Caroline, at Social Services,' she said, and he couldn't help noticing how her eyes sparkled, and she was smiling. 'They're having a very difficult time finding a fosterer to take Hope.'

'Oh?' He gave her a sideways glance as she came up beside him to watch him change Hope's nappy.

'She explained that there had been a fall-off of people volunteering to foster over the past two years. And at this time of the year, with Christmas so close, it's even harder than usual to find a foster parent at short notice.'

Theo didn't even think about it. As he turned to face Nya, Hope in his arms, he said, 'I'll foster her. For at least as long as I'm on leave from the hospital. That'll give them a chance to find her mother, or a permanent fosterer.'

'Oh…' Nya exhaled, and her smile faded away. It was as though she deflated right in front of his eyes.

'What is it?' he asked, resting a hand on her arm when she would have stepped aside, and holding her gaze.

'Oh, it's just that…'

When she hesitated, Theo joggled her arm. 'Tell me.'

Her eyes glittered, and he realised it was tears making them gleam.

'Well, I was planning to foster Hope myself.'

She was holding herself stiffly, and tried to look unconcerned, but although the moisture had disappeared from her eyes, he could easily see she was still upset and trying not to show it.

'Here.' He motioned for her to take Hope from him, and Nya didn't hesitate. In a trice she had the infant snuggled close. 'Sit down, and let's discuss this.'

'I don't know that there's anything to talk about,' she said as she walked to the armchair and subsided into it. 'You're actually a better choice than I am. I can't take holidays now, because I have a trainee, a new midwife, and we're one midwife short too. You fostering Hope makes far more sense.'

She was right, but seeing Nya's tender expression as she looked down at a relaxed and cooing Hope, he knew not fostering the baby would be a huge disappointment to his friend.

'We could share the position as Hope's fosterers,' he said, again without giving it any thought, but he knew he'd made the best suggestion when her face lit up.

'I'd love that. If you don't mind? I can have her at night, and you can look after her during the day, while I'm working.'

Time to tread gently here. Knowing Nya's strength of will, he didn't want to put her back up.

'Are you sure you'll be able to get enough sleep, if you have her at night?'

Nya hardly spared him a glance.

'Single mums do it all the time. I'll be fine. Besides, I rarely sleep more than four or five hours a night.'

'I didn't know that.'

That brought her head up, and she gave him a wide grin. 'You've only known me for twenty years. Normally, you'd only get that type of information after twenty-five. This constitutes special circumstances.'

He couldn't help chuckling, and it occurred to him that he hadn't laughed as much in ages as he had today.

'So, is it that you don't go to bed until late, or do you wake up extremely early?'

'It depends. Sometimes, if I've had a particularly hard day, I'll go to bed early—by ten. Otherwise, I'm up until at least midnight.'

Theo nodded. 'I'm something of a night owl myself,' he admitted. 'But if you find yourself getting sleep deprived, just let me know and I'll take Hope for a night or two.'

'I'll have some days off during the time leading up to Christmas, and I can catch up on sleep then.'

She was smiling again—almost glowing—and Theo couldn't take his eyes off her face.

'That's settled, then,' he said, earning another of her wide grins. 'I'll call Caroline and let her know what we've decided—that we'll share the care of Hope until at least the end of the year. I'm sure she'll have a mountain of paperwork she'll need us to fill out.'

'Normally the last thing I want to do,' Nya said, smiling at Hope and stroking one chubby baby cheek with the backs of her fingers. 'But I'll gladly do it for you, sweetheart.'

And the warmth that filled Theo's chest felt so good, he ignored the little voice in the back of his mind, telling him to be careful of what he was getting into.

That one round of heartache was more than enough, and he was definitely courting another.

By the time they'd got all the legal details dealt with, it was getting late, so Theo said he'd call down to The Dolphin and ask the publican Davy Trewelyn to send dinner up for them.

'Lovely,' she told him, casting an eye over the pile of nappies, babygrows, wipes, and other necessaries, ticking things off the list in her head. 'By the time you get home, you won't want to have to cook.'

'And you won't have time to,' he replied in that low sing-song voice that let her know he was talking to Hope rather than her. 'Right, Hope?'

'Tomorrow I'll get a car seat for her on my lunchtime,' she said. 'Thankfully Marnie said she wasn't planning to take Violet anywhere tomorrow, and we could borrow hers tonight. And the carrycot from the nursery here will do as a place for her to sleep tonight too, but it will make sense for both of us to have one, rather than have to take it back and forth.'

'Don't worry about that,' Theo told her.

'Give me a list and I'll order everything on-line tonight for one-day delivery.'

'You don't have to—'

Theo held up his hand and shook his head.

'Just let me buy my girl some things, please? I want to.'

It was on the tip of her tongue to warn him not to get attached—that this was a temporary situation—but he looked so happy and appealing, Nya kept the thought to herself.

Besides, she was having just as hard a time reminding herself of that fact too.

Since she'd walked to work that morning, after they'd eaten they packed everything into Theo's car, and he drove her and Hope to her cottage. Nya had used the app on her phone to turn on some lights at home, including her outdoor Christmas lights, and as they drew up she cast a critical eye over the modest display.

'I need more decorations outside, I think,' she said to Theo as he switched off the engine. 'Somehow each year I end up doing less than the year before. Or I suddenly can't find strings of lights I was sure I had and get frustrated.'

'It looks lovely,' he replied as he opened his door. 'Very cheery indeed.'

'Have you put up your decorations yet?'

she asked, opening her door as well so as to swing her legs out.

'No. I haven't got around to it.'

If voices could have a 'keep out' sign attached, Theo's did just then. The way his voice cooled had her wondering if there was more to the story than just not having time to deal with the holidays yet.

Going into the cottage in front of him, carrying Hope in the borrowed car seat, she directed him where to put the packages. Then she bustled about, putting supplies away in an orderly way, so she knew where to find them.

'Who knew that one tiny baby could need so many things?' she said, stifling a giggle. 'I never thought I'd need more counter space in my lifetime.'

Theo smiled and shook his head. 'It does look like a lot, doesn't it?'

Hope chose that moment to awaken, and before Nya could go to her, Theo was there, lifting her from the carrier, checking whether it was a nappy change or feeding time again.

Nya stayed where she was, watching him, wondering why her heartbeat was suddenly so erratic, and tingles were firing along her spine at the sight of the pair.

Then she gave herself a mental shake.

It had been an emotional day—at least for

her. And now she had the wonderful prospect of taking care of Hope for a month or so, until a permanent fosterer or her parents could be found, to look forward to. No wonder she was feeling a little gooey on the inside at the sight of a handsome man holding a tiny baby.

Almost any woman would, wouldn't they?

Theo was almost finished changing Hope's nappy, and although Nya was assailed with the wish that he didn't have to go, she forced herself to say, 'We have to remember to put the car-seat base into my car, so I have it for the morning. What time should I bring Hope over to you?'

He sent her a glance over his shoulder and shrugged. 'Whenever you get there will be fine. I'm usually up early to go for a run, but if I know you're coming before eight, I'll stay home.'

Suddenly the image of him in running attire popped into her head, sending a rush of heat out through her veins, and it took a moment to get her brain back into working order.

'No…no. Go for your run. My first appointment is at nine, so I'll bring her by at about eight-fifteen.'

All too soon he was handing her Hope and taking her car keys so as to transfer the car-seat base, and then coming back in to take his leave.

Hope was starting to fuss a bit, ready for her next feed, so Theo didn't linger.

'See you both in the morning,' he said, before bending to kiss the top of Hope's head.

Then, before Nya realised what was happening, his lips—warm and firm, yet wonderfully soft—were on her cheek, seeming to linger on her skin for an eon, before he straightened.

Something in his eyes had her heart galloping along like a runaway horse, and all she could do was stare up at him, until he suddenly swung around and headed for the door.

Finding her voice, she called, 'Night,' and got a wave in return.

Then he was gone.

As she was warming Hope's bottle, Nya thought back on the day and the roller coaster of emotions she'd been on.

Jim, and Mum, and Hope, and Theo. Each played a role. But Nya's head kept taking her back to that moment when she'd seen Theo come through the door at Carey House, and the way her body had reacted.

It was just *Theo*, after all. Long-time friend and co-worker.

A man obviously struggling with everything life had thrown at him over the last couple of years.

Someone she wanted to see happy again, instead of so often stern and sad.

Hope spat out the nipple, then rooted about for it again, making Nya giggle. It seemed the baby's favourite trick.

'There you go,' she said, lining it up for her again, making encouraging noises as the infant went back to her bottle.

Once upon a time, so long ago now it seemed just a dream, she and Jim had talked about the children they hoped to have. Two boys, he'd insisted, so they'd have each other to torment and fight with, and at least three girls.

When she'd laughingly asked him why three, Jim had said, 'Because then they can take turns looking after me when I'm in my dotage, and when one gets tired of my tricks, she can send me off to the next.'

She'd agreed, even as she'd shaken her head at the thought. Five children were too many, in her book, but since all that childbearing had then been in the future, it had been easy to go along with him.

And of course, none of that had happened. When she'd lost Jim, the thought of children had been put aside. She couldn't envision herself parenting with anyone other than him—had never even really tried to find another relationship. He had been one of a kind, but when she'd said as much to her mother, Iona had shaken her head and given Nya a stern look.

'Each of us is one of a kind, and different. If you spend your time trying to find another Jim, you're going to be sorely disappointed. Look for—find—another one-of-a-kind man who will love you differently, but just as much. You deserve that.'

'I don't want anyone else,' she'd replied, which had led to that heated discussion between them. And the unspoken agreement not to speak about it any more that Mum had broken earlier in the day.

A welter of emotions washed through her as she rocked Hope and let her thoughts wander where they would, seeking some kind of peace and clarity, both of which proved elusive.

'Oh, Jim,' she whispered finally, shaking her head. 'How I miss you still.'

But that night, after she got Hope settled and climbed into her own bed, it was Theo Turner's face that floated up into her mind and followed her into slumber.

CHAPTER FIVE

JUST BEFORE DAWN next morning, Theo pounded along the narrow lanes surrounding his home, determinedly getting the exercise he knew he needed but despised having to get. Every time he went for a run, it reminded him of his age and the swift passage of time.

When he was young, he'd played football and been a keen cricketer, but once he'd got to university he'd stopped playing regularly because he could no longer commit to a team schedule. Yet, although that was many years ago, he still considered those team sports the only exercise worth doing.

Running or jogging was rather boring, and really gave him far too much time to think.

And no matter what he started thinking about, he ended up on one subject.

Nya.

Her warm smile and gorgeous, soft skin

that suddenly, after all these years, made his fingers tingle with the urge to touch.

The tenderness she showed to Hope. Her gentleness as she stroked over the baby's head or cheek.

He was used to her brisk common sense, the way she always made him feel heard and appreciated, but noticing these other, far more personal things had his brain spinning.

Was this just another side effect of the life changes he'd gone through?

He'd be the first to admit he'd been terribly lonely. While he'd always thought it was his responsibility, not only to support and encourage his children, but also prepare them for adulthood, it had been a wrench when they'd left home. And once they had, the cracks in his marriage had widened until there was no way to traverse them.

When Femi had left, it had been almost a relief. A surcease of the constant arguments interspersed with cold silences.

At first the peace had been soothing, but then the emptiness of the cottage and his apartment in Falmouth had begun to register.

And the peaceful feeling had drained away, making him not want to go home after work.

Last night, as he'd looked around Nya's cosy living room, decorated for Christmas, he'd realised just how cold and sterile his own place was. Nya's personality was obvious everywhere——her warmth and humour clear in the colourful decorative items, the festive baubles——and, strangely, he'd felt his attraction to her go up a notch. It all had made him want to pull her to sit down on the sofa beside him, cuddle her and Hope close to his side, and find a kind of sweet oblivion.

Of course, he had done no such thing.

While there had been a couple of times yesterday he'd caught Nya looking at him in a way that made his heart race, there was no way to know exactly what she was thinking. Suspecting he wasn't alone in this new awareness didn't make it so, no matter how the idea interested him.

No doubt that was why, as he got to the next crossroads and looped back, he got a little spurt of additional energy as he realised Nya would be dropping Hope off soon.

Trying to distract himself, he went over the list of things he'd accomplished the night before.

Ordered probably more things for Hope than she'd ever need, but he'd been enjoying himself so much that he'd ended up deciding on gifts for TJ and Gillian too.

That had led him to think about what Nya

had said about people being responsible for their own happiness, and admit to himself that he was allowing the past to shadow the present. Calling his children had seemed appropriate then, and their conversations had further soothed his soul.

'Since I'm stuck here until the day before Christmas Eve finishing this collaborative project, I was hoping to come down to Carey Cove between Christmas and New Year,' TJ had said. 'But only if it's no bother.'

'It will never be a bother for you to come home, whenever you want,' Theo said, surprised but trying not to show it. 'But I thought you were spending the hols with your mum.'

There was a pause, and then his son said, 'Yeah, I said I would, but I wanted to figure out if you'd be around, should I decide to come down to see you.'

Theo knew his son well, and could put two and two together. Femi would never outright lie to their children, but she was expert at hinting at things, leaving them open to interpretation. Just as she'd hinted to Theo that the children had no interest in spending the holiday with him, she probably did the same to them by insinuating Theo had no time for them.

'Oh, I'm not going anywhere,' he replied, feeling more cheerful than he had in ages.

Gillian had apologised for not having enough time off to visit, adding that she was spending the following Christmas in Carey Cove, no matter what.

Intellectually he knew his children loved him, but hearing evidence of it made all the difference in the world.

And when he'd told them about Hope, and his offer to co-foster her with Nya, they'd expressed their approval, although Gillian had teased, 'What, Dad? Didn't think you could manage a baby all on your own?'

'Shut it, you,' he'd replied, as Gillian had hooted with laughter. 'I offered, but Nya looked so disappointed—because she'd wanted to foster the baby herself—that I suggested we share.'

'Ah, I see,' she'd replied slowly. 'Well, that's good, then.'

But when he'd asked her to elaborate, she'd brushed him off and changed the subject, leaving him wondering whether his children would be pleased or annoyed if he got involved with Nya.

And there he went again, thinking about Nya as he jogged up the driveway towards his door.

But if he was hoping for some indication that she'd felt the same rush of interest as he had the day before, he was quickly disillusioned.

She was her usual brisk, bustling self when she dropped Hope off, but even more so, since she whirled through his front hall like a tornado, depositing supplies. Bringing him up to speed about how the baby had slept, and how often she'd fed, as she transferred the car-seat base to his car. And then, after kissing the top of Hope's head, she headed right back out of the door, leaving him feeling as though he'd been run over by a small but determined lorry.

'Well,' he murmured to Hope, watching Nya's car turn onto the road. 'That'll teach me to misinterpret things, won't it?'

And Hope made a sound that he swore was half amused, half sympathetic, and he couldn't help laughing, even though there was no mistaking his disappointment.

Nya found herself speeding away from Theo's house and eased off the accelerator. She was flustered, just from seeing him, catching a hint of his fresh, soapy scent. It had made her imagine him in the shower after his run, his body slick with water, the suds running down a stark contrast to the darkness of his skin.

The fantasy caused a rush of desire she was desperate to hide from Theo, and the best way was to retreat behind her work persona. But even then she wasn't sure she'd been completely successful, since her heart was racing and she felt slightly breathless by the time she got back into her car.

'Get a hold on yourself, Nya,' she muttered, turning the car into the driveway of Carey House. 'You don't have to see him again until the end of the day.'

But her heart did another of those silly lurches at the thought, and she still felt off-kilter as she went inside.

Thankfully it was home-visit day, and having Lorna the trainee midwife with her forced Nya to keep her mind on work and off Theo Turner.

At least until they got to Marnie's to check on her and baby Violet.

'So tell me everything,' Marnie said as Nya supervised Lorna's wellness check of Violet. 'About Theo finding a baby on the doorstep of Carey House, and how both of you are taking care of her. I didn't have time to chat when I dropped the car seat off with you yesterday, but now I want to hear the entire story.'

Just hearing Theo's name made Nya start, and that gained her a surprised glance from Lorna.

'Oh…er…' Nya stopped talking to say to Lorna, 'Remember to make notes as you go along. Don't try to commit anything to memory. Well-kept records will aid parents and medical practitioners alike going forward.'

'Yes, Mrs Ademi—I mean Nya,' Lorna said, obviously remembering that Nya insisted they be on a first-name basis. As she then turned her attention to noting Violet's length and weight, saying them out loud, she thankfully gave Nya a chance to recover her equilibrium.

But she knew Marnie had noticed her reaction, and it took all her focus to smile and tell the younger woman about Hope. Even then, Nya concentrated on telling Marnie about the evening before, when the baby was with her, rather than the rest of the day when Theo had shared the responsibility.

Then, once Lorna was finished with Violet, Nya pulled her into the conversation and, to her relief, Marnie turned her attention to the young trainee, grilling her about her plans. While they chatted, Nya held Violet, who was just a few weeks older than Hope. It came to mind how, once upon a time, she'd dreamed of raising her children alongside those of her friends, but of course that wasn't to be.

If Hope were to stay in Carey Cove—stay with Nya—she would grow up with Violet and have a built-in best friend and pseudo cousin.

Over the years she'd come to accept her childless state, and it was no longer a source of pain. However, today she felt a pang as she reminded herself that her custody of Hope was only temporary. Even if they didn't find her mother, Social Services would find a permanent fosterer, and that was all there was to it.

But it was surprisingly easy to drift off into a fantasy where she and Theo were together, raising Hope. Living together, sleeping together...

'Isn't that right, Nya?'

It was only when Marnie nudged her that Nya realised she'd missed the entire conversation, and heat rushed to her already warm face.

'Umm... What?'

Marnie's eyes narrowed, and she looked as though she was about to say something, but then she glanced Lorna's way, and just shook her head, saying, 'Never mind. What else do you ladies have on the schedule today?'

Taking the reprieve in both hands, Nya smiled, replying, 'Why? Are you missing the hustle and bustle already?'

'I am, in a way,' she said with a laugh. 'But I'm enjoying my new job too much to leave it just yet.' Violet chose that moment to start to fuss, and Nya handed her back to her mum with a grin, as Marnie tacked on, 'No matter how demanding my new employer is.'

Lorna and she left not long after that, heading back to the clinic.

As they drove along, Lorna said, 'That layette set you made for Violet is lovely, Mrs Ademi—I mean, Nya. Where did you get the pattern?'

Nya glanced at the young woman as she replied, 'From my mother, who has a huge collection. Do you knit?'

'A little,' Lorna admitted. 'But I get frustrated, I'm that slow. I'm far better at crochet.'

'We have a fibre arts group here in the village, if you're interested. We usually get together once a month to chat, share patterns, drink tea or wine or, if you're Mrs Haymore, a vodka martini.'

'Oh!' Lorna sat up straighter and Nya knew the trainee was looking at her. 'I noticed the postbox topper outside the village shop, and the tree on the green wrapped to look like an angel. Did one of you make them?'

Nya tapped the side of her nose, grinning. 'The first rule of yarn bombing is—'

'Don't talk about yarn bombing,' they finished together, and they were laughing as she turned back into the drive at Carey House.

Nya was telling Lorna more about the club and some of the projects they'd done over the years as they walked into Reception and saw a little crowd of people around Hazel's desk. And in the midst of them, Theo, holding Hope.

It was impossible to ignore the way her heart flipped, and then started galloping. Thankfully Theo hadn't noticed her yet, so Nya had the chance to both feast her eyes and also compose herself. Yet, the latter was difficult.

Theo looked so handsome, so comfortable and proud holding Hope and showing her off to the midwives, patients and Hazel that Nya almost couldn't stand it.

Just once it would be nice to see Theo unkempt, or as frazzled as Nya felt just looking at him. Oh, she knew just how very human he was, but just now, with this new awareness of him sending carnal shivers through her body, she wished he'd put a foot wrong in some way. Maybe that would break the spell.

Then, as she hesitated just inside the door, Theo looked up and saw her, and his smile just about knocked her over.

Suddenly there was a flurry of motion, as all the midwives with patients escorted them away, and the others vanished too, as though Nya were poison. It happened so quickly it was almost cartoonish, and between her rush of pleasure at seeing Theo's smile and her amusement a giggle broke through before she could stop it.

Who knew she was scary enough to have that kind of effect on people? Luckily Theo didn't seem to feel the same way, because he was walking towards her, that gorgeous smile still in place.

'There you are. We came to ask you to join us for lunch.'

'I'd love to,' she said instinctively, but then added, 'But Hope's too young to be going to the pub. In fact, she shouldn't be around so many people yet. We don't know anything about the circumstances of her birth, her health, or her mother's. We don't even know if she was born in a hospital.'

Theo nodded, not losing his smile. 'Yes, I fended everyone off as best I could. And I thought we could order out and either eat in my office here, or at my house.' Before she could reply, he held up his hand, continuing, 'I know you've been doing home visits, and Hazel said you usually bring lunch from home, but I doubt you had time to make much of anything this morning.'

Nya was very aware of Hazel sitting at her desk, no doubt listening intently to their conversation, and was glad when the phone rang, and she had to answer.

'I'd love to,' she said again, 'but—'

'Nya, Dr Turner.' Hazel was always unflappable, but Nya recognised the note of urgency in her voice and swung around. 'Liz McDermott is suffering excruciating back pain. Her husband wants to know what to do.'

'Tell him to bring her in, immediately.'

It was Theo who answered, and Hazel nodded, taking her hand away from the receiver to tell Kyle McDermott what had been said.

Turning to Theo, Nya said, 'Placental abruption,' making it a statement, rather than a question. Liz had been under Theo's care for the last two months, closely monitored since the partial abruption had first been diagnosed. Liz had been on bed-rest and was almost full term now, but the danger to both mother and baby if the abruption had progressed was still very real. 'I'll prepare for ultrasound, and the delivery room.'

'Contact Roman too,' Theo said, striding across the room. 'We may need to airlift Liz to St Isolde's for an emergency C-section, depending on what we find.'

It was all hands on deck then.

Hazel took charge of Hope, while Nya found Lorna in the staff room, and had her assist in setting up the ultrasound machine, and laying out everything they'd need, including instruments for a caesarean, just in case.

'I'm sure you remember from your classes that placental abruption is when the placenta begins to detach from the uterine wall.' Nya brought Lorna up to speed as they worked, so her trainee would be prepared by the time the patient was brought in. 'Liz McDermott, a twenty-six-year-old first-time mother, came in two months ago for a routine check-up, and reported light, intermittent vaginal bleeding. She was thirty-one weeks along. Our GP, Dr Wilde, diagnosed the *abruptio placentae* and referred Mrs McDermott to Dr Turner. Dr Turner recommended bed-rest, and both Mr and Mrs McDermott were given a list of symptoms to look out for.'

As she spoke she was mentally double-checking the room, making sure Theo would have everything to hand if and when needed.

Then came the sound of voices down the corridor, Liz's shrill with fear, and Theo's soothing tones.

With one last look around, Nya turned to Lorna, who looked a little worried. No wonder. This was Lorna's first placement, and she'd been honest about her lack of experience.

Nya smiled, and bumped the younger woman with her elbow.

'You'll be fine. Just follow Dr Turner's lead. And get the door.'

CHAPTER SIX

THEO'S EXAMINATION AND the ultrasound determined that Liz's abruption had grown larger.

'I'm going to induce labour, Liz. It's time to get this little fellow out.'

'All right,' she said, looking terrified and hanging onto her husband's hand so tightly his fingertips were turning white. 'Is the baby doing well?'

'We're monitoring him carefully,' Nya told her. 'Don't worry.'

After Theo had administered the oxytocin, he took Nya aside.

'Have Hazel call and get Roman on his way here. I want to make sure that if there are any complications after delivery, Liz and her son will be on the way to St Isolde's for treatment as soon as possible.'

Nya nodded, and slipped from the room to do as told. The chances of haemorrhage and clotting issues after an abruption were high, and although the baby was near term, he might still have issues with his lungs.

Liz's labour started in earnest not too long after, and in quick time her son was born. Just then Nya heard the distinctive *wump-wump-wump* of the helicopter's rotors, as Roman brought the aircraft in for a landing in the field behind the hospital.

Baby McDermott gave a weak wail as Nya placed him briefly on his mother's chest, and both parents cried with relief at seeing him.

Then she had to break up the tender scene, taking the infant for a quick check of his Apgar score, glad that Theo had arranged for transport.

'Seven on the Apgar,' she told Theo quietly. 'With a one on the A, G, and R.'

He nodded tersely. 'I'm going with them to Falmouth. Let's get them ready for transport.'

After a flurry of activity, soon Roman was wheeling mother and baby to the helicopter, Theo walking alongside the gurney, holding Liz's hand.

As the helicopter rose into the afternoon sky, Lorna sighed.

'Think they'll be all right, Nya?'

Putting an arm around the younger woman's shoulders, Nya gave her a brief hug.

'There are no guarantees, but I think so.

Beside the fact that St Isolde's is a first-class hospital, Dr Turner is one of the best obstetric consultants around.'

Making their way back into the hospital, they parted company—Lorna going off to salvage what she could of her long-abandoned lunch, and Nya to go and collect Hope.

'Oh, do let me keep her here with me.' Hazel, always so motherly, was clearly enjoying the task of babysitter. 'I haven't had a baby to cuddle for ages. Besides, you're still on shift, aren't you?'

Nya laughed, and waggled her fingers in a *give it here* motion.

'I don't often pull rank, but what's the use of being Head of Midwifery if I can't occasionally skive off to take care of my foster baby? If anyone needs me, I'll be in my office. And if there's another emergency, I'll bring her back to you.'

With an exaggerated sigh, Hazel handed Hope over, and Nya set off for her office, going via the staff room to collect the container of salad she'd thrown together that morning.

Hope was awake, but not fussing. Nya checked her nappy anyway, and settled her in her carrycot before tucking into her lunch.

Thank goodness today was Saturday, and

senior midwife Sophie was on call for Sunday, while Nya took the next two days off. That meant Nya had time to take care of Hope and still get some of her usual chores done. She'd been meaning to tell Theo she'd keep Hope tomorrow and the next day, so he didn't need to worry, but, somehow, she hadn't got around to it.

And she knew why.

Until she could figure out what these feelings and reactions she was having whenever he was around were, she was determined to minimise contact. Yet, wouldn't that mean telling him not to worry about taking care of the baby for the next two days, so there was no need to see him? Instead of doing that this morning, when she'd thought of it, she'd blithely gone on with her day. After all, she could easily have texted him after she'd dropped Hope off…

Tearing her thoughts away from that particular conundrum, she pulled out her phone and brought up the app she used to make her to-do lists.

The last one she'd made a couple of days ago still had a number of chores on it, and she quickly picked out the ones she deemed most important. Laundry. Finishing the ruana she was knitting for her mother, and the last of the lap blankets she was planning to donate to the care home in Penzance. Putting up the last of the decorations in the cottage and finding time to deal with her super-secret project.

Then there were new items to add.

A layette set for Hope.

Maybe a gift for Theo?

Leaning back in her chair, she gave that some thought.

Since she'd never given him a Christmas gift before, except for once when she drew his name for the work Secret Santa, wouldn't doing so now seem strange?

Yet, at the same time, they were friends of long standing, and co-fosterers now too. Wouldn't *not* giving him a gift seem even stranger?

Should she invite him to spend Christmas and Kwanzaa with her, Mum and Hope? She had no idea what his plans were, or if he'd even be interested in coming to her cottage on the day. Maybe he was thinking of having Hope to himself, unless TJ and Gillian were coming down to spend the holidays with him?

She'd have to ask him, and that was all there was to it, since that was the only way to find out. Adding asking him his plans to her list didn't solve the question of the gift though, and Nya didn't like not having her ducks in a row.

'Don't be daft, Nya,' she scolded herself, rubbing her temple. 'Ask him about his plans, *then* decide about the gift.'

But there was no way to avoid the knowledge that she hoped he'd want to spend the day with her. With them, she corrected, even as she grimaced and admitted she'd got it right the first time.

She wanted to spend time with him, even as she dreaded it too. Whatever was happening with her, she knew it was one-sided and, if she were smart, she'd never let Theo figure out how her feelings towards him were morphing.

It was probably just a temporary thing—an anomaly brought on by the time of the year, and the shared experience of caring for Hope.

Besides, there was no telling whether Hope would still be with them at Christmas time, she reminded herself firmly. The social worker had intimated that unless they found the baby's parents, she probably would be, but Nya knew she had to brace herself for whatever came.

In the past, the first part of December had always been an off time for her. Jim's birthday, coupled with the Christmas festivities rushing towards her, had often made her feel off-kilter. It had taken a number of years after his death for her to genuinely enjoy the holiday season again. He'd loved it so. Insisting on dressing as Santa Claus and handing out gifts at the base party, even though it took pounds of stuffing to achieve the proper dimensions. Buying his mum and dad the very best gifts he could afford, and watching with such joy when they opened them.

Showering her with presents too, even when she scolded him for spending so much of his money. He'd just laugh, and pick her up to spin her around until she was dizzy, threatening not to stop until she admitted she liked them. Making her laugh so hard, as she clung to his neck, that tears rolled down her cheeks.

Such a zest for life.

Mum's words came back to her, lingered in her mind, as she closed the app, and picked back up her fork.

Loving Jim had taught her to enjoy whatever came her way.

Losing him had taught her nothing lasted for ever, and it was wise not to get too invested in anyone.

All things, especially good things, came to an end.

And, for once, she was glad to have her

phone ring in the midst of her lunch, since it put paid to her muddled, somewhat maudlin thoughts.

'Hello. Nya Ademi,' she said briskly into the phone.

'Hi, it's Caroline Harker. I was just calling to see how things were going with baby Hope, and to tell you I've made an appointment with the paediatrician on staff with us to have a look at her next Tuesday. Will you be able to take her to Penzance then?'

'Of course. Just tell me the time, and either I or Dr Turner will make sure she's there.'

By the time she'd got off the phone, having taken all the details, and despite what she'd said to Hazel, it was time to get back to work.

Luckily the afternoon wasn't particularly busy, but what with Nya supervising Lorna and seeing patients, Hope spent more time with Hazel than Nya would have liked. All the comings and goings around the reception area made it a less than optimal environment for such a young baby, even though Hazel made sure to keep everyone at bay.

Except herself, of course.

'She's such a little darling, isn't she?' she cooed, as she once more reluctantly handed Hope over to Nya at the end of the day. 'Such a good baby too.'

'She is,' Nya agreed as she strapped Hope into the car seat in preparation for the trip home. Unfortunately, the base was still in Theo's car, and the keys were presumably in his pocket. Luckily, Nya's cottage wasn't too far, and she'd decided to walk home rather than risk driving with the untethered carrier. 'She really only cries when she's hungry or needs a fresh nappy. Otherwise, she's just as happy as can be.'

'My youngest seemed to never stop crying,' Hazel said with a laugh. 'Came out wailing like a banshee and didn't stop until she turned twenty or so.'

'I'll make sure to tell her you said that the next time I see her,' Nya replied, trying to make it sound like a threat, even though she couldn't help giggling. 'I'm sure she'd enjoy hearing it.'

'Oh, she'd give me an earful, for sure. Off with you, before you get me into trouble.'

Although still early it was dark outside, but the streetlights were on, and although it had drizzled earlier and a light mist hung in the air, the walk home wasn't unpleasant. Most of the cottages visible from the street were festooned with lights, and here and there a Christmas tree twinkled behind the windows. Nya took a deep breath of crisp air, grateful that the day was coming to a close, and she had two days of loving up on Hope to look forward to without interruption.

Drat it. She still hadn't texted Theo about that.

Shrugging to herself, she decided to do it after she'd got home, and settled Hope for the night.

As though on cue, as soon as she got to her door, Hope stirred, and let out an exploratory cry, which Nya now recognised as the preamble to her *I'm hungry...feed me now* wail.

'Just a few minutes,' she said, giggling as she got the door open. 'Your timing is impeccable.'

This was, she thought a while later, her new favourite time of day. Hope was fed and bathed, exuding that sweet, heart-melting baby scent as Nya held her on her shoulder and rocked her to sleep. She couldn't remember a more peaceful time, or one that made her feel as though she were exactly where she was supposed to be. So much so that it took a great deal of determination to finally get up and take Hope to her cot, and put her down to sleep.

Wandering back out into the living room, Nya stood still for a moment, contemplating whether to bother eating or not. Really, she didn't feel like cooking, and crackers and cheese didn't appeal. As though in objection to the thought, her stomach rumbled.

'Crackers and cheese it is, then,' she said aloud, heading for the kitchen.

Then headlights swung across the glass pane at the front of the house, and she paused. The sound of the car's engine shutting off had her walking to peep out through the window, in time to see Theo getting out of the vehicle.

Even as her heart did that ridiculous thing it had taken to doing whenever she saw him, Nya was trying to reason with herself, and get her breathing under control.

He must have just stopped by to bring the car-seat base. That was all.

She stepped back from the window, giving herself just a few seconds before opening the door.

Theo indeed had the base for the car seat in one hand, and in the other was a paper sack.

'Sorry for leaving you without use of the seat,' he said, with one of those heart-melting smiles. Holding up the sack, he continued, 'I brought dinner, as a peace offering.'

'Not necessary,' she replied, stepping back so he could come in. 'But gratefully received. I was just about to have crackers and cheese, not wanting to bother cooking.'

'Not the most nutritious way to end the day, but I completely understand. I've had a few nights like that myself.'

Funny how her perfectly adequate home, with its open living and dining room combination, suddenly seemed to shrink when Theo entered. He took up all the space, and apparently more than his fair share of the air, since Nya still had to fight to catch a deep breath.

'I'll get cutlery,' she said, for the sake of something to say. 'Sit down.'

Setting the bag down on the dining table, he started taking out containers, and Nya's stomach rumbled again at the heavenly scents suddenly filling the air.

'I wasn't sure what you'd like, but I stopped at the Ethiopian place in Penzance, since I know their food is always good.'

Nya felt a giggle rising in her throat, and bit it back.

'You must have been talking to my mum. She loves that restaurant.'

She was coming back out of the kitchen as she spoke, and saw his head tilt slightly, before he replied, 'You know, I think it was Iona who told me about it, months ago.'

'I'm not surprised. She'd eat there every night if she could. How are Liz and her son?'

Theo was unwrapping a foil packet, those lovely hands deftly opening it without tearing either the covering or the injera within.

'She's stable and should make a full recovery. We needed to cauterise and give her blood, and little Nicolas will be in the NICU at least until tomorrow, to make sure his lungs are functioning properly.'

'Yum,' she said, as he opened a container and the familiar scent made her mouth water. '*Doro wat*. My favourite.'

Theo smiled, and she had to look away.

'Many kinds of *wat*,' he said. 'Since I wanted to make sure there was something you'd be happy to eat.'

They used the plates, but the cutlery remained pristine as they both ate in Ethiopian style—tearing off pieces of injera and using the bits to scoop up mouthfuls of the various stews.

Conversation was restricted to requests to pass each other dishes, as they both ate hungrily. When they were finished, Nya got up to put away the leftovers, while Theo asked to look in on Hope.

'Of course. Last door at the end of the hall.'

And she turned towards the kitchen, not wanting him to see how the thought of hav-

ing him in her bedroom made her face feel
as though it were on fire.

All she could hope was that by the time
she went to bed, there'd be no trace of Theo's
distinctive scent lingering there, to bedevil
her dreams!

CHAPTER SEVEN

NYA'S BEDROOM WAS something of a surprise,
and yet very much like her. Bright and cheerful, eclectic yet quite traditional when it came
to the furniture and patterns.

Somehow, knowing how Afro-centric
her mother was, Theo had half expected the
décor to lean in that direction. But, rather,
William Morris-esque curtains, mid-century
modern furniture, and pops of colour pro-
claimed that Nya's style was whatever she
happened to like, rather than a set pattern.

He liked it. A lot.

Even though entering into what was her
private space also gave him more of those
untoward thoughts he was continually battling whenever they were together. His eyes
gravitated towards her neatly made bed, and
he quickly jerked them away, looking instead
at the cot.

Hope was fast asleep, and hadn't even

stirred when he turned on the light. Going to stand over her, Theo touched her cheek, then her tightly curled fist, with one finger. How tiny and vulnerable she looked and was. His heart ached each time he thought about what might become of her.

Even if they found her mother, would the woman be fit to take back her baby, or would Hope end up one of the hundreds of children entering the foster system? Staying in it until they aged out. Never knowing a truly loving home.

A part of him wanted to rail at the thought. To swear it would never happen on his watch. Yet, he knew, in this case, he had no real power over the situation. Whatever was to happen, he'd have to wait and see.

Knowing there were no answers to be found tonight, he bent to press a kiss to Hope's hair, and turned to leave the room.

A picture on the bedside table caught his eye, and he paused, staring at it.

This, then, was Nya's husband, James. Jim, she'd always called him, the few times she'd spoken of him in Theo's presence.

A tall, well-built man, broad of shoulders and thick of neck. Obviously in perfect physical shape, if this full-body shot was anything to go by. Dressed in his army uniform, he could have been an overawing sight, except for the absolute delight on his face as he grinned at the camera.

Nya usually gave one of her delicious little giggles when she talked about him. He was, she'd once said, a man who never seemed to have a bad day. He brought joy and laughter with him wherever he went.

Why looking at the picture made Theo's chest tighten was inexplicable, and when he turned away to exit the room, he couldn't help glancing back once more, before he turned off the light.

Trying hard to battle a sudden surge of resentment against a man simply because he was loved so deeply, and for so long.

'Still sleeping peacefully?' Nya asked as Theo walked back into the living room, having paused in the hall to compose himself.

'Like the little angel she is,' he replied, wondering why he was so reluctant to say goodnight and go home. Of course, it was because he had nothing to rush home *for*, did he?

'Sit down. Can I offer you a cuppa? Or a drink?'

Suddenly relieved that she wasn't kicking him out just yet, he opted for a cup of tea. When he moved back towards the dining table, she waved him towards the fireplace instead.

'Can you put a match to that for me? It's getting cool in here, and a fire will make sure Hope doesn't get a chill.'

'Funny how things have changed over the years, isn't it? Before the 1990s, the norm was cover baby with a blanket, put her on her stomach, and leave all her stuffed toys in the crib with her. Nowadays, it's dress baby warmly and put her to sleep on her back with nothing whatsoever in the crib.'

Nya made a little sound of assent in her throat.

'Everything changes, especially in light of new research. How are Gillian and TJ? Are they coming for Christmas?'

He didn't look up from the fireplace, glad she wouldn't be able to read his expression.

'Not this year.' He hesitated, and then decided he might as well tell her the rest. 'I don't know if you heard, but Femi got married a couple of months ago. She and her new husband are having a big family get-together, and TJ and Gillian will be going to that.'

Nya didn't comment right away, but he heard the rattle of teacups and pot as she walked back into the room.

Putting the tray down on the occasional

table in front of the love-seat, she sat down, and he thought he could feel her gaze on him, making a little shiver run down his spine.

'I didn't know about her marriage.' Thank goodness there was no sympathy in her tone, just a deeply contemplative note. 'I tried to reach out to her a few times since she left, but she never replied, so I stopped. Well, if you don't have any plans, you can spend Christmas with Mum and me. And Hope, of course, if she's still here.'

Her thoughtfulness made him smile, and feel able to get up and face her, instead of hiding.

'I'd like that. Especially if Hope is still in our care. It'll be her first Christmas, and she deserves a good one.'

The fractional tightening of the skin around her eyes was the only indication of anything untoward, since her mouth was still smiling, but he knew how she felt. He didn't want to contemplate giving up Hope either, although he knew they'd have to, eventually.

Wanting to take Nya's mind off the subject, he heard himself say, 'You know, when I think back on all the holidays I missed with my children, I really regret it now. I let my work consume me, to their detriment.'

Her eyes widened. 'But surely you don't believe that's true?'

'It is true.' Sitting down beside her on the love-seat, he turned slightly so he was facing her, his arm along the back. It wasn't the largest couch in the world, and he was suddenly aware of the heat of her leg against his, the proximity of her hair to his hand.

If he could have shifted away without it being obvious, he probably would have, but since that wasn't an option, he held still.

'Why do you think so, Theo?'

When she looked at him like that, with that clear-sighted gaze, he felt as though he would tell her anything she wanted to know.

Even his deepest shame.

'I know it's true, because I lived it. I was so determined to make sure they had everything they needed—stability, financial security, someone showing them how to be a productive citizen of the world—that I sacrificed my home life.'

She tilted her head. 'But those things are important. Why should you feel guilty about providing them?'

'Yes, they are important, and I know that because it's the complete opposite to how I grew up. My father was a shiftless bastard, who rarely worked. And when he did get a job, he spent all his money drinking and gambling. I promised myself I'd never turn out that way, and worked hard to make sure of it.'

Even to his ears his voice sounded choppy—uneven—but he couldn't stop the spate of words.

'That I'd never endanger my family by putting my pleasures before their needs. But there's a line between being successful and letting that success be everything in your life, and I crossed it.'

Nya's lips pursed, and when she leaned forward to pour the tea, he wished he could see her face.

'And what's your relationship with them like now?'

'Good,' he said, surprised at what he thought was a change of subject. 'I spoke to them just last night. TJ wants to come and visit between Christmas and New Year, if he can manage it. The engineering degree he's taking at Cambridge is intensive, but his marks have been amazing.'

'And Gillian?'

He couldn't stop the smile that took over his face as he took the proffered cup from Nya's hand.

'She's doing brilliantly. She's working for a fertility clinic in London as a researcher, but I think she may opt to go back to school to become a doctor eventually.'

Nya took a sip of tea, her eyes downcast. Then, when she lowered the cup and turned to look at him, he was surprised at the tenderness in her gaze.

'Theo, stop being so darn hard on yourself. You've helped to raise two wonderful young people, who love and admire you. Can't you give yourself credit for that?' Before he could respond, she raised her hand to stop him, and a soft smile tipped the edges of her mouth. 'I don't know if you realise, but my father died when I was eleven, and Mum raised me by herself. Now, you think you're driven? I wager my mum would run circles around you in that respect. She was determined to get a professorship, and was always studying and writing books to make that happen. Then it was getting the university to create an African studies course. She was determined and focused but, at the same time, she was raising me. It wasn't always a successful combination.'

She was smiling, but he felt his heart clench. He wanted to know how that had affected her, but the words stuck in his throat, fear of what she might say keeping them there.

Nya took another sip of her tea, then reached to put the cup down, before she continued.

'Yes, there were times when I resented her not being at home, or was hurt when she'd missed a special occasion at school, but I also always knew she was *there*. Available to me if I needed her. And she was the very, very best role model I could have ever had. She taught me that if you want something, you have to work hard for it, and sacrifice too, if that's what was necessary.

'Your children know you're there for them. They watched you work hard and strive to make their lives comfortable—to give them the opportunities they're enjoying now. I know I saw you at rugby matches, and at concerts in the hall when they were performing. If you were as much of an absentee father as you seemed to think, you wouldn't have bothered with any of that, so cut yourself some slack.'

Her words, coupled with that sweet, gentle look in her eyes, made his heart swell, and then begin to race. Unable to resist, he touched her cheek with the back of his hand, and almost groaned at the softness of her skin.

He wanted to thank her, to tell her how

much he'd needed to hear what she'd said. How suddenly free he felt, as though she'd let loose a rope that had been slowly squeezing the life out of him, allowing him—for the first time in months—to take a deep, cleansing breath.

But none of those words emerged from his mouth, because by then he was too busy kissing her, and all thoughts of talking fled.

Nya didn't move, as Theo's lips touched down on hers, but her immobility lasted only for a moment. Then her arms went up around his neck, and she was pulling him closer, deepening the kiss herself, as need exploded out into every vein and muscle in her body.

She'd tried so hard not to imagine what it would be like to kiss Theo, but now she had to acknowledge that no matter what she might have come up with, it would never have been enough.

His lips were softer than she'd have imagined.

Their firmness and mastery couldn't have been dreamt up accurately.

The first sweep of his tongue across the seam of her mouth was hotter, slicker, more arousing than any fantasy could ever be.

Was this what they meant when they talked

about melting into someone's arms? It felt like it, as her skin grew hot and so sensitive that when Theo's hand curved around her nape, it sent energy surging into her trembling belly.

He gentled the pressure on her mouth fractionally, sucking on her lower lip, nipping at it with his teeth, and there was no stopping her moan of desire.

Then the kiss turned wild, a frantic tangle of tongues, as their breath rushed and her heart beat so hard and fast, she could hear it in her ears.

He leaned forward, tilting her back against the arm of the love-seat, and she didn't resist, wanting to know where this was going. Wanting to feel the hard press of his body against hers.

Wanting him in a way she'd never wanted before.

And then, a shrill wail rent the air, and they both froze.

Instinctively, Nya's hands fell to Theo's heaving chest and pushed. Immediately he pulled back, his arms falling from around her, leaving her suddenly cold. And as she stumbled to her feet, she realised she was shaking from head to toes.

Theo's hand came up, as though to steady her, and she sidestepped out of reach. She should say something—make a pithy comment or something trite—but nothing sensible came to mind, so she did the only thing she could think of.

She fled to the bedroom to scoop up the crying infant and hug her close.

'You're okay, sweetie. There's a good girl,' she crooned, hearing the wavering in her voice. Her tension must have transmitted itself to Hope, since the little girl stiffened and cried harder, rather than relaxing the way she usually would.

Taking deep breaths, Nya rocked Hope, trying to get her own heart rate down. It wasn't time for a feed yet, so once Hope calmed a little, Nya quickly laid her down and changed her nappy.

Hope stopped crying, and Nya was contemplating if she had the nerve to go back into the living room, when she heard the unmistakable sound of her front door closing and knew Theo had slipped away.

Blowing out a long, hard breath, she plunked down on the end of her bed, putting Hope on her shoulder in her favourite position for falling asleep.

She'd kissed Theo.

Theo!

And not just kissed him but enjoyed it in a way that left her shaken and aroused, aching for the type of physical contact she hadn't had—or wanted—in ages.

Closing her eyes, she relived the moments, imagined it continuing, becoming more intimate.

Theo's hands and mouth exploring her body, touching and slipping, increasing her need until it reached fever-pitch…

Pulling her thoughts back from where they'd so wantonly taken her was far too difficult, but Nya knew she couldn't afford to let them stray too far along that path.

None of this was or could be real. Theo was going through a difficult time, and no matter who objected, or thought she should move on, her heart belonged to Jim, and no one else.

Theo and her being thrown into close proximity because of their shared care of Hope, at this particular time in their lives, had created an anomalous situation. Once things went back to normal, they'd both be left considering what on earth they'd been thinking, kissing like that.

It was wrong—for both of them—but as

she lay down on her bed, still cuddling Hope and looking at Jim's picture, she wondered why it felt so very right all the same.

CHAPTER EIGHT

IT WASN'T UNTIL the next morning that Nya remembered she hadn't spoken to Theo about not having Hope that day or the next. She was dithering between calling and texting him when her phone rang, and her heart tumbled over itself before she realised it was her mother calling.

'Morning, Mum,' she said, hoping her breathlessness wouldn't be too apparent. 'How was the seminar?'

'It was lovely, but what's this I hear about you fostering a baby?'

Trust her mother to come straight to the point, once the minimum of niceties was out of the way. Nya couldn't help giggling.

'So, you already heard. That'll teach you to go haring off to Penzance and leave me to my own devices.'

Her mother's snort spoke volumes.

'Tell me everything, from the beginning.

I've only got dribs and drabs through the grapevine.'

Nya did as she was told, outlining for her mum all that had happened the last two days, trying to make it all sound quite normal and banal. Yet, each time she had to say Theo's name, her heart missed a beat, and she was worried it affected her tone of voice.

A fear that seemed to be borne out when, after she was finished, her mother asked, 'So, you and Theo are sharing custody of little Hope? That's…interesting.'

'No, Mum,' Nya quickly interjected. When heard that way it sounded too intimate, as though they were creating a family together. 'We're temporary co-fosterers. Just until they either find her mother or can arrange for a permanent foster situation.'

Nya could usually interpret the sounds her mother made, but this time she didn't even want to.

'Well, I'm looking forward to meeting Hope soon. From what you've said, she'll be with us through Christmas, yes? Have you asked Theo to join us?'

'Yes. Unless they find Hope's mum, she'll be with us until the new year. I told the social worker I'd keep her at least that long, so they didn't have to fuss about finding a fosterer before then. And, yes, I did invite Theo to join us.'

Why did that last bit feel like making a concession?

'Good. And please invite him to our Kwanzaa celebrations too.'

'I'll tell him about it, Mum.' Nya glanced at her watch. If she didn't contact Theo soon, he might turn up on her doorstep. 'But I have to go. I think I hear Hope stirring.'

'When do I get to meet her?'

Just her luck that this morning, when she was eager to get off the phone, Mum wanted a bit of a chat.

'She's only a week or so old, so I'm trying to limit her exposure to new people for a little while more. But you're family, so why don't you let me know when you're free, and I'll bring her by?'

'This afternoon will be wonderful,' Mum said promptly. 'Come for tea. I'll wear a mask when I'm holding the baby.'

Nya shook her head, but couldn't help smiling. It was impossible to get annoyed with her mother's high-handed ways, simply because she saw it for what it was—a way to navigate a world that hadn't always been kind. Iona had built a no-nonsense persona to not just ensure she got what she wanted, but also as a barrier against disappointment.

'Oh,' Iona continued, before Nya could respond to the invitation. 'Bring Theo with you. I always enjoy his company.'

Then she hung up.

Theo.

Without time to consider whether to text or call, she brought up his number and pressed call.

And heard his phone ringing outside her door.

Darn it. Too late.

A soft knock sounded just as he answered, and she could hear the laughter in his voice as he said, 'Hullo. Fancy letting me in?'

'Let me think about it,' she replied, feeling a bit silly as she patted her hair like a schoolgirl getting ready to see her crush.

She tried to pull herself together, but his soft chuckle sent a shiver through her, and she felt even giddier as he said, 'I brought gifts.'

'Are you Greek?'

'Not the last time I checked. And I don't have any horses with me.'

Opening the door, she shook her head. 'You better not have. My back garden isn't that big, and it's a little early to be buying Hope a pony.'

His grin made her heart soar as he bent to pick up the pile of boxes at his feet, and she stepped back to let him in.

'Oh, I don't know. It's something to think about.'

He put down the boxes, then promptly turned and went back outside for more. Nya watched him, torn between amusement and that silly, flustered sensation.

'You might not have bought her a pony, but this looks like a pony's weight in things. What is all this?'

'Just a few things I thought Hope needed.' He looked so ridiculously pleased with himself, Nya's heart—already doing little somersaults—absolutely melted. 'I found a car seat that comes with two bases, so we can each have one in our car, and give Marnie back hers. Then there are blankets, bibs, babygrows, towels...'

He was pulling things out of boxes as he spoke, and Nya put a hand over her mouth to stifle the giggle rising in her throat. Theo paused and skewered her with a look.

'Why do you always do that?' he asked, gesturing to her hand. 'Muffle your laughter?'

She didn't think anyone had ever noticed that habit she had, and it made her feel a bit self-conscious. But not wanting him to know, she wrinkled her nose and replied, 'It's silly, the way I laugh. I sound like a twelve-year-old, rather than a mature woman.'

Theo's eyes narrowed. 'Whoever told you that is a twit. I love the way you laugh. Every time I hear it, it makes me smile.'

Heat rushed to her face, and Nya turned away so he wouldn't see how his words affected her.

She'd been teased about her laugh since secondary school, and had actively started trying to hold it back in nursing school. Once she'd started rising in her job, she'd felt it undermined her authority and really tamped it down.

Pretending to survey the stack of boxes, she said, 'It's a good thing it's wash day for me. All of this lot—barring the car seat, of course—will need to be sanitised before we can use them.' More in control now, she glanced over at him, and made sure not to get snagged by his gaze again. 'I had planned to tell you that you didn't have to come and get Hope today. That I'd be happy to do the Sunday/Monday shift, since I'm off tomorrow too.'

'Oh, no, you don't.' He sounded amused, but there was a hint of steel in his voice too.

'You're not depriving me of Hope's company, and yourself of a chance to get some well-deserved rest.'

'I don't mind. She's so good, and I have some chores to do here, and then I promised Mum to take Hope around to see her, so if you have things to do—'

'The only thing I have to do is take care of Hope.' He sounded so firm Nya knew he wasn't budging. 'So, if you want me to just hang about here until it's time to go to your mum's, I can do that too. That way if you want to nap or just not have to stop whatever it is you're doing, I'm here keeping things under control.'

If she made a fuss about it, he'd surmise their kiss the night before had changed their relationship, and Nya wasn't willing to have that happen. So, although everything inside was screaming that she shouldn't spend any more time with Theo than was absolutely necessary, she gave in.

Throwing her hands up, she huffed. 'Okay, then. Have you had breakfast?'

Both of them couldn't fit comfortably in her little kitchen, so it would be a good way to put a little distance between them.

'I had a protein shake.'

Trying to get back the teasing atmosphere

they'd achieved when he'd just arrived, she said, 'Is that how you keep your schoolgirl figure?'

Theo actually looked shame-faced, as he replied, 'Actually, the truth is that I'm a terrible cook. Really terrible.'

She couldn't suppress her giggles, but found breath enough to say, 'I very much doubt that's true. You're far too competent a human being not to be able to boil an egg and make some toast.'

Which led him into a hilarious story about burning a meal on the outdoor grill, making Nya laugh until tears filled her eyes.

But it was the sense of relief that things were back to the way they were—before his divorce, and definitely before that kiss—that made her light-hearted.

Having spent most of the previous night reliving their kiss, and trying to figure what, if anything to do about it, Theo had come to the conclusion that it was an anomaly best left unremarked.

At least, he assumed that was what it was for Nya. And her determined effort to get rid of him at first, and then to keep the atmosphere light when he made it plain he wasn't going, seemed to bear it out.

She wanted him to know she wasn't interested in him physically, but still wanted to be his friend, for which he was overwhelmingly grateful.

As for how he viewed their kiss…

That was where things became far less clear-cut.

Not only had holding her felt amazing, and kissing her been mind-blowingly arousing, but it had all felt…somehow…

Right.

As though somewhere in his subconscious he'd been waiting for the chance to hold Nya, taste her lips, know what it felt like to be touched by those soft, capable hands.

Which was absurd.

He'd taken his marriage vows seriously. It had never, ever occurred to him to be unfaithful by look or thought. So he was quite sure he'd never thought of Nya that way, at all. Yet, there was no mistaking the sheer delight he'd experienced the night before.

Which had brought a rush of guilt and confusion that had kept him up, pacing the house late into the night.

Since his marriage fell apart, both friends and family members had urged him to start dating, but he hadn't been interested. His whole persona had been built on focus and stability—being responsible and committed to whatever he was involved in. While mentally he accepted his failure to hold his family together, emotionally it was difficult to break the chains. Dating had felt like cheating—an attitude he knew would eventually hold him back, but hadn't seemed something to worry too much about in the short term.

And his response to even that brief intimacy with Nya showed he was right. Even if there hadn't been the issue of Nya being his friend, and seemingly determined not to get involved with anyone, he wasn't ready either.

Maybe, like her, he'd never be.

Which made her attitude and reception this morning something to be thankful for. It felt as though he'd lost so much over the last eighteen months, it would be devastating to lose Nya's friendship too.

Leaning on her kitchen doorframe, he kept their conversation light, even though he was hyper-aware of her every move as she bustled about making breakfast. When he heard Hope stir, he went to get her, before Nya had a chance to do more than look up.

The one thing he was determined to do today was make sure Nya had all the help she needed, whether she wanted it or not.

After changing the baby, he took her into

the kitchen to find that her bottle was already in the warmer.

'I could have done that,' he said.

Nya gave a little snort and rolled her eyes. 'I was already in here and I know where everything is. It would have been silly to make Hope wait while you fumbled around, when it took me all of two seconds.'

'Do you hear how she talks to me, Hope?' He turned the infant, who was making unhappy sounds but not yet crying, so they were face to face, her little body easily fitting between his hands. Hope's gaze seemed to focus on his, enthralling him totally. 'You'd think she'd be nicer to us, wouldn't you?'

He glanced up in time to see Nya's nose go up in the air. 'I'm always nice. Don't you be turning my baby against me.'

For Theo time seemed to slow, almost stop. The way she said it, the ease of the atmosphere, was like home. Home the way he'd always dreamed it could be, but never actually was.

Then he pushed the thought away.

He and Nya had always had a bantering relationship, both at work and in social situations. There was nothing new or strange about this morning, except that there was precious Hope added to the mix.

And, considering the way he'd been avoiding Nya since the divorce, having the infant throw them together, reigniting their old friendship, made it all extra precious.

Best not to make too much more of it.

So he went back to teasing, as he fed Hope and ate his breakfast, feigning annoyance when Nya, in turn, twitted him about his ability to do both at the same time.

The day flew along, but with an effortless flow Theo found entirely enjoyable. He'd bought a knapsack-type carrier, and put Hope in it so he could help Nya hang clothes on the line in the backyard. They'd had a spate of nice, sunny weather, cool enough to need a light jacket, but the wind, which had been blustery over the last few days had died down.

In the same vein as before, Nya said, 'Well, you're a champion washer man. You obviously know your way around a clothes line.'

She was so easy to talk to, he found himself explaining, 'My mum worked two or three jobs when we were young so, being the oldest, I had to figure out how to keep things going at home when she wasn't around.'

Nya sent him a questioning look. 'Had your father left, and she'd become a single mum?'

'No.' Even after all these years, he couldn't

keep the derision out of his voice. 'She would probably have been better off if she had been. My father wasn't interested in doing anything around the house, although he hardly worked. Mum kept the trains running mostly by herself in those days.'

She was silent for a moment, and then asked, 'I remember meeting her once, about five years ago. She lives in America, doesn't she? I don't remember meeting your father, though.'

Harder now, but he didn't feel the need to retreat from the conversation the way he usually would.

'Yes, Mum lives in San Francisco with her second husband—an American she met when he was stationed at the embassy here, but the last time she visited she was on her own. I have no idea if Dad is alive or not. He divorced Mum just about the time I started uni, and never looked back.'

'I'm sorry.' It sounded as if she was, although he appreciated the brisk way she said it. 'That must have been hard on you all.'

He paused, the clothes peg in his hand hovering above the line, and waited for the anger, but somehow when it came it was more subdued than usual.

'I think it was more of a relief than anything else.' The words came slowly, and it felt somehow *good* to say them. 'I know Mum was hurt by it, because she'd tried so hard, and stuck it out no matter how difficult it became. But I thought it was the best thing that could have happened. The situation was wearing her down, you know? Making her old before her time. She's a lot happier now.'

Nya made a little sound of acknowledgement in her throat. 'It's so heartbreaking, watching someone you love go through the tough times, and there's nothing you can do to make it better.'

The way she said it was like putting a full stop at the end of a sentence, and Theo was more than happy to change the subject thereafter, asking her what time she was due at her mother's.

'She likes to have tea at four, and you're invited, if you'd like to come.'

It was on the tip of his tongue to refuse, but instead he instinctively said, 'I'd like that.'

Then wondered what that sideways glance she gave him meant.

'I have something to do afterwards, but it's a secret. Can I count on you not to say anything?'

Intrigued, he said, 'Of course. What is it you're up to?'

There came that lovely giggle, and a teasing, arched-brow look.

'You'll see. Later.'

And no amount of prying could get it out of her.

CHAPTER NINE

NYA KNEW SHE'D be a fool not to be worried about going to her mother's house with Theo. Mum was an astute observer, who far too often noticed things other people missed, and didn't hesitate to comment. Yet, to her surprise, Mum said nothing untoward, and seemed too wrapped up with Hope to perhaps notice the change in her daughter.

And Nya was sure there must be some outward signs of the turmoil raging inside.

Oh, she thought she did a good job pretending the easy relationship she'd always had with Theo was unchanged, but she knew it was just a façade. Her heightened awareness of him, and the way her gaze was constantly drawn back to him, made her self-conscious. She spent much of the visit trying to find anywhere else to look, rather than at him, and with her fingers fisted, so as not to touch him in passing.

Telling herself it was just the after-effects of their kiss the night before didn't help. In fact, it made it worse, because it brought their embrace back to mind, and caused crazy waves of heat to rush from her torso into her face.

But somehow she got through tea with a smile on her face, and when Mum suggested they bring Hope to visit again the following day, did her best to dodge the invitation.

'Theo will have Hope tomorrow, Mum,' she said, knowing she was contradicting what she'd said to Theo earlier, about being willing to take care of the infant the next day herself. 'And I'm sure he has other plans.'

'I don't actually.' Theo smiled, looking so adorable with Hope nestled against his chest in the carrier, Nya could hardly stand it. 'I just planned to hang about. Maybe tutor Hope on the finer points of football while we watch a match or two that I've missed today.'

'In that case, definitely bring her back here,' Mum said, the laughter in her eyes belying the acerbic tone of her voice. 'I'll have to counteract that with a discussion about Beowulf and the beauty of Old English literature.'

Theo laughed as he bent to kiss Iona's

cheek, and Nya shook her head at the two of them, although she couldn't help laughing too.

'That was nice,' Theo said as they set off walking back to Nya's cottage. 'I really like your mother a lot. She's always interesting.'

Nya laughed, only just stopping herself from muffling the sound with her hand. 'You mean colourful?'

Theo's eyes glinted with laughter. 'She is that, but no, that's not what I meant.' His lips pursed for a moment, as though he was trying to find the right words. 'Iona always struck me as the type of person who doesn't give her trust or friendship easily, but once you've earned it, it's immovable. That's something I can appreciate.'

'You're rather like that too,' she said, although the realisation surprised her in a way. 'But without Mum's sharp edges.'

Theo shrugged one shoulder, tipping his head back to look up at the moon, which was waxing and, although not yet full, lit up the lane. His profile was rendered sharp by the play of light and shadows, and as Christmas lights flashed colours across his dark skin, she found him heartbreakingly handsome.

'I learned to be careful of people, to recognise that not everyone will have my best interests at heart. But, at the same time, I actually like most of the folks I meet. I'm just not willing to let everyone into my inner circle.'

She nodded, hearing the self-reflection in his words, appreciating his candour.

'Mum's life hasn't always been easy,' she replied. 'And I think that's another thing you have in common too.'

He slanted her a look from beneath lowered lids, his lips twisting slightly, before relaxing into a smile again.

'Maybe. I'd never really been one to self-analyse, but for the last year I feel as though it's almost all I've done, when I'm not work-ing. And I still don't have any answers.'

They were at the corner of the high street now, and she stopped him with a hand on his arm, unable to resist touching him.

Just in sympathy, she told herself, as she would have done at any time at all during their long friendship.

'Sometimes you have to accept there aren't any easy answers, and sometimes no answers at all.' Then, because the air around them felt too heavy, and she was fighting the urge to tug him close and kiss him again, she let go of his arm, and said, 'Are you ready for our secret mission?'

His teeth flashed as he grinned. 'What are you up to?'

'Come this way, and you'll see.'

When she turned up the road, away from her cottage, he followed. There were a few people on the high street, and from the sounds of it The Dolphin pub was full, but the farther they got from it, the quieter it became.

'Are we going to the hospital?' he asked.

'Shush,' she said, looking around as they approached the postbox near the entrance to Carey House. 'We're stopping here.'

'What are you up to?' He spoke quietly, as though her surreptitious behaviour had infected him.

'You'll see.'

The postbox topper was the first she'd ever crocheted, and she was quite proud of it. She'd created a retro winter scene of a pond partially ringed by trees, with couples in Victorian costumes skating on the surface. Around the edge she'd attached holiday-themed ornaments that dangled down on ribbons.

Definitely over the top, but hopefully worth the effort.

Pulling it out of the bag, she carefully fitted it over the top of the box, heaving a sigh of relief when it actually fitted properly, and the trees and figures stood up without drooping.

When she stepped back to look at it, Theo was close by her side, and when he put an arm around her shoulder, she couldn't bring herself to move away.

'That's beautiful.' He sounded enthralled. 'And impressive. But why…?'

'Let's get out of here,' she replied. 'I can't be seen in the vicinity. I'll explain later.'

Then, setting a brisk pace, but trying not to look too conspicuous, she led the way back towards home.

'It's called yarn bombing,' she said, once they were far enough away, and there was no one around. 'It's a type of street art, not illegal, but sometimes frowned on by the powers that be. The ladies of our fibre arts group have been doing it for a few years. You must have seen some of our work around the place.'

'I have, and always thought they brought a bright spot to the streets. Why would it be frowned on?'

'Well, it's sometimes seen as a nuisance—not as bad as graffiti, but in the same vein. Usually, though, they leave it up for a while, especially when it's close to Remembrance

Day, and the artwork is military or poppy themed. As long as it isn't impeding the public in some way, the council here in Carey Cove doesn't seem to mind.'

'So, why all the cloak and dagger, then?'

He was laughing at her, a bit, but she liked that better than the solemn and stern Theo she'd been used to seeing recently.

'Well, half the fun is in leaving everyone guessing who actually did it. This time, no one will think it's me.'

'Why not?'

They were turning into her driveway then, and she knew, suddenly, she didn't want the night to end just yet. Without looking at him, she said, 'Because I'm known as a knitter, not a crocheter.'

He chuckled softly, the sound tickling down her spine, making her shiver. 'You know I don't have a clue what the difference is, right? But I'll take your word for it, and promise not to spill your secret.'

'Thank you.' At the door now, before she lost her nerve, she said, 'I'm going to bathe Hope when I go in. Would you like to help?'

'I would,' he said, in a calm tone that nonetheless sent a little shiver along her spine. 'Thank you.'

'You're welcome.' Her fingers felt a little

unsteady as she fitted the key into the door, and she took a deep, silent breath to get them under control. Hopefully she wouldn't eventually regret the invitation, but just then, as they walked into her living room, all she felt was elated.

Nya turned on her Christmas tree, bathing the house in twinkling lights, reminding Theo of how very sterile his own home looked.

'I should put up some decorations,' he said as Nya helped get Hope out of the carrier. 'Every time I see yours I think so, then I just forget about it.'

'And get a Christmas tree.' Nya laughed up at him, her dark eyes sparkling. 'Do it for Hope, if you won't do it for yourself.'

'Of course,' he replied, laughing with her. Feeling ridiculously happy to be with her and Hope, and invited to participate in the evening ritual. 'I'm sure Hope will appreciate a tree.'

It wasn't until they were at the kitchen sink, Hope kicking her little legs on the counter while he undressed her, that Theo realised the close quarters he'd be in with Nya during the bath.

Too close, he thought, as his arm brushed

the side of Nya's breast and his breath hitched momentarily in his chest.

Steady on.

But even while concentrating on undressing the squirming Hope, his awareness of Nya kept growing.

A soft scent he recognised as purely her own.

The sight of her capable hands as they moved to turn the water on and off and gather the supplies closer to the sink.

Her body's warmth, which seemed to reach out to him.

And every time their bodies touched, a bloom of heat spread from the spot, until his entire body vibrated with warmth.

Desire.

'Here we go,' Nya said gently, reaching over to pick up Hope so as to place her on the rubber sink liner. Hope's eyes opened wide for a moment when she was submerged in the water, and then her little legs and arms started waving back and forth. 'Oh, you love your baths, don't you, sweetie?'

He didn't know exactly what the emotion was that overtook him, but the backs of his eyes prickled, and his voice came out a little roughly when he said, 'I'll hold her for you, and you wash.'

'Thank you.'

They fell into a rhythm that only served to increase the sense of intimacy enveloping them in Theo's mind. Working together to wash Hope's hair, both of them leaning close, so from the corner of his eye he could see the smooth curve of Nya's cheek. He searched for a topic of conversation that would put some emotional distance between them, and decided it would help to remind himself of Nya's unavailability. Maybe that would dissipate this growing longing tightening his muscles and making him light-headed.

'May I ask you a very personal question?' he asked, not really sure whether he wanted her to answer yes or no.

'Of course,' she replied, still in that sing-song voice she used with Hope, but he saw the way she shot him a quick sideways glance. 'Anything.'

'Why did you never remarry?'

The hand wielding the washcloth paused for an instant, and then resumed its gentle stroking.

'Do you know, I don't think anyone has asked me that so bluntly before.'

'I'm sorry,' he said quickly, but she shook her head.

'Don't be. It's better than people just assuming they know and giving me unsolicited opinions.' She was quiet for a beat, and then continued, 'The short answer is that I never found anyone who made me *want* to get married again.'

'And the long answer?'

'Could you sit her up, just a little, for me, please?' He did as she asked, holding Hope up so Nya could wash the little back easier. 'The long answer is that when Jim died, I was so devastated it took me two years to think about him without crying. He'd always warned me that with him being in the army the possibility of his death in action was very real, but I was too young, too inexperienced to believe it would happen. And staying in Andover was too painful. I'd see a uniform in the distance, and my heart would leap, and then break again when it hit me that it wasn't Jim.

'Would never again be Jim.'

She paused, leaving Theo wondering if that was all she would say, but then she sighed, and shook her head slightly.

'Coming back to Carey Cove was an effort to seek comfort. Being closer to Mum, seeing familiar faces and visiting old haunts helped me heal, but it was never meant to be permanent. I always thought at some point I'd be "ready".' She put down the washcloth and used soapy fingers to do air quotes. 'Then I'd leave again and move on with my life. But somehow months turned to years, comfort turned to comfortable, and when my career was going so well, it felt like a sign, and I put any other plans aside.'

'So it wasn't that you consciously decided not to marry again—just that the opportunity never presented itself?'

'Something like that.' The little snort she gave wasn't quite laughter, but it was close. 'Carey Cove isn't crawling with eligible men, and the times I go to Falmouth or Penzance, it's not to party or go to clubs. I've dated a little over the years, but that brings me right back to where I started—with not finding anyone who could make me feel even a fraction of what I felt for Jim.'

He'd been right. This was a subject that helped get his head back on straight.

Obviously, Nya had been so intensely in love with her husband that no one had ever been able to compete. He'd even heard Hazel mention that December first was Jim's birthday, which was why Nya had taken the day off. Probably to visit his grave.

Realistically, who could compete with a

man who would, in Nya's mind, always remain young, full of joy and life?

Nya had turned aside to pick up the towel she'd placed close to hand, and Theo let out a silent breath, keeping his focus on Hope, who looked relaxed and sleepy after her bath.

Here was someone whose life he could make a real difference in, even if it were for just a short time. And he needed to remember it was all for a little while—that no matter how homey and lovely being with Nya and Hope felt, it wouldn't last.

Remembering that was the only way to save himself from further heartbreak, and he was determined to do just that.

Yet there was no mistaking the tender ache around his heart as he watched Nya wrap Hope in the towel. Telling himself it would be wise to leave to return to his own life didn't work, and it was only when Nya went towards her bedroom with Hope that he realised he couldn't stay a moment more.

The intimacy of going into that room with Nya, to be under the laughing stare of her beloved husband, felt like too much to bear just then.

Even so, it took considerable strength of will to make his goodbyes, and leave the lovely warmth of the cottage behind.

CHAPTER TEN

NYA FELT THAT life was settling into a dangerous routine, but there was nothing she could do to change it—even had she wanted to.

Both she and Theo had taken on the responsibility of caring for Hope, and if that brought them together in a way Nya knew was dangerous to her peace of mind, what was she to do?

Over the following days Theo would appear at her door in the mornings and, depending on what each of them had planned, either picked up Hope or came with Nya to Carey House. Each lunchtime he would appear, either with a meal from the pub that they'd share at Nya's desk or with a picnic if the weather looked nice enough for Hope to be outside.

In the evenings, he lingered at Nya's cottage, helping her to feed and bathe Hope and invariably having dinner too. Some nights he seemed reluctant to leave, and Nya could understand that. Living alone, after being used to having his family around him, had to be difficult.

Making sure not to sit on the love-seat with him again—not because she didn't want to invite his kisses, but because she worried she'd grab and kiss *him*—Nya would take out her knitting.

And that was when she had to forcefully remind herself how temporary all of this was. It felt so cosy and natural to have him there. They drank tea and discussed everything from world affairs to the doings around Carey Cove—like how Don Mitchell had fallen from a ladder while putting up more decorations.

'I'm quite sure he was trying to outdo Kiara's display,' Nya told Theo with a shake of her head. 'But all he's accomplished is a broken leg and worrying his family. You know their daughter, Tara, is heavily pregnant, and I heard she's insisting on coming from Milton Keynes to check on her dad.'

'Poor Avis must be beside herself,' he replied. 'Now she'll not only have Don and the kennels to worry about, but Tara too.'

So like him to be concerned about others. Moments like that just intensified Nya's sense of him belonging in her cottage. In her life. By the third night, she almost found herself asking if he were ready for bed, as though he lived there, rather than had his own place to go to.

On the Tuesday, Nya took a few hours off, and they travelled together to Penzance to take Hope to her doctor's appointment.

'All seems well,' Dr Miller told them, after a comprehensive examination. 'She's a bit on the smaller end of the height and weight scale, but not as though she was premature. You mentioned that over the last couple of days she's been a bit stuffy, but her chest sounds clear. Because we don't have any information on her mother, birth, or first days of life, I'd suggest keeping a sharp eye for any infections or illness. Otherwise, it seems as though, between you, you're doing a marvellous job.'

She hadn't been able to stop herself from grinning over at Theo, and when he grinned back, she was once more struck with the sense of family, and of rightness.

Dangerous indeed, she reminded herself later that night as she lay in bed, and even looking at Jim's picture didn't make the feeling fade.

'You look like a couple,' her mum said,

thankfully quietly into Nya's ear, as they were all together for the lighting of the village Christmas tree later in the week.

Nya thought about laughing but, realising she couldn't manage to make it sound natural, she gave her mother a stern look instead, and a shake of the head.

'We're just friends, Mum. You know that. Please don't do anything to make it awkward.'

That earned her a twist of her mother's lips, and one of her high-handed glares. 'I would never do anything inappropriate, Nya. I just made an observation.'

And, thankfully, Mum left it at that, although Nya was sure there was lots more she really wanted to say.

The night was surprisingly warm and dry, and the village green was filled with people. Davy and Darleen Trewelyn from The Dolphin Inn had set up a tent where they were dispensing mulled wine, hot chocolate and cider. Across the way, Kiara's amazing Christmas display eclipsed every other attempt at decorations, and all the children lined up to have their pictures taken in Santa's sleigh.

Hope, snug in the carrier against Nya's chest, was awake and chewing on one fist, and Theo, who had gone to get them all drinks, was making his way slowly back towards them. Every few steps, someone would stop him for a chat, and Nya smiled to see how relaxed he looked.

How happy.

Even with her mother's words still ringing in her ears, warning her again that she was getting into deep waters, Nya couldn't help wishing that she'd been the one to bring that smile to his face.

Finally getting to them, Theo said, 'Sorry it took so long. Hopefully your drinks aren't cold.'

He handed Iona her mulled wine first, and then stepped close to Nya. So close that his arm rested against hers, and when he bent his head, he could speak right into her ear.

'There's a spirited, almost combative discussion happening near the tent regarding who put up the postbox cover near Carey House.'

He sounded so amused Nya had to laugh too, as she took her hot chocolate from his hand. 'Did they mention anyone you know?'

'Several people, but not you.'

She laughed again, a little breathlessly now, because having him this close seemed to steal the air from her lungs.

'I'm pleased to hear it.'

Someone called out to him, and Theo straightened and turned to answer. Nya was still smiling when she met her mother's gaze, and Iona's lifted eyebrows seemed to clearly say, *Really? Just friends?*

All Nya could do was throw her mum a narrow-eyed glare and turn away, hoping that the heat filling her cheeks wasn't obvious.

The tree was lit, amidst cheers, and a round of carols was sung with gusto. At Theo's insistence, they made their way over to Kiara's display and climbed onto the sleigh to have their picture taken with Hope, Mum standing at the side, beaming.

When Hope began to fuss, Nya said, 'Time to head home, I think. She's been a doll but it's getting too chilly for her to be out much longer, especially with that snuffy nose of hers.'

'I'm going to stay a bit longer,' Mum said. 'Lisa has been wanting to start a book club over the winter, and I promised I'd give her some suggestions.'

'Okay, Mum.' Nya leaned in for her mother's kiss, and wasn't surprised when, after kissing her daughter's cheek, Iona pressed her lips to the top of Hope's head too.

As Mum walked away, Nya turned to Theo

to say, 'You can stay too, if you like. We'll be fine walking back alone.'

Theo snorted, and didn't bother to reply, unless you considered slinging an arm around her shoulders and guiding her away from the crowd an answer.

'Actually, I wanted to ask you a favour,' he said, when they were on the pavement and heading towards her cottage.

'What is it?'

His arm was still around her shoulders, and although she thought she should pull away, she couldn't bring herself to do so. It just felt so good.

'I still haven't put up my decorations. If I offer you dinner tomorrow evening, would you be willing to help? I'll be the first to say decorating isn't my forte.'

'Sure,' she replied, trying to match his casual tone, but inside already looking forward to it. 'Instead of you bringing Hope to me, I'll come over to yours after work.'

'Excellent. I promise not to cook for you.'

'Thank you,' she teased. 'I appreciate that.'

When his hand cupped the back of her neck, she swore his palm heated her nape, even through her coat collar and light scarf.

'If you don't behave,' he growled, 'I'll be forced to break out my grill.'

She had to swallow against her suddenly dry throat and fight a threatening shiver, forcing herself to maintain the casual banter.

'Oh, no! Anything but that!'

And somehow she kept the jovial atmosphere going all the way to her front door. When she unlocked the door and stepped inside, she was surprised to realise Theo had stopped on the threshold.

'Aren't you coming in?' she asked, as she looked down to unbuckle the carrier, and then eased Hope out. When she looked up, the expression on Theo's face made her freeze, the breath catching in her throat.

Then he looked down for a moment, and said, 'Not tonight. I'm going to head home.' With a smile that didn't quite reach his eyes, along with a wave of his fingers, he turned away to stride off into the night.

Just as well, she thought a little shakily as she closed the door behind him. If he'd stayed, she might have been tempted to kiss him again, and she couldn't afford to go down that road.

Not if she wanted to maintain their friendship, her pride and sanity.

Theo knew if he'd gone back into that warm, cosy cottage with Nya and Hope, spent another evening with them, as though they were family, he wouldn't be able to resist.

Resist the draw of Nya's smile, her shining gaze, her lush, sassy mouth.

The urge to pretend he could belong again and start over.

Walking away had been a wrench, but necessary, so as not to make a fool of himself, and risk the friendship he had with Nya. Yet, the following morning, as he looked out of his kitchen window at the light drizzle, he still regretted doing it, and wondered if inviting her over this evening was wise too.

He wanted her, with an intensity he found difficult to comprehend and was still trying to come to terms with and understand.

Was it just a case of rebound on his part? Loneliness?

A result of his long sexual drought?

Or was there something more there? An emotional connection that went beyond that all-important friendship?

Until he could figure that out, he wouldn't chance losing the relationship they did have, on a whim.

And, even if there was something more on his side, would Nya ever be willing to explore it?

She'd always seemed happy—content—

with her life. Safely ensconced behind the bastion of her widowhood. Remembering a love that would never age, or change, or wither.

In a strange and stupid way, he envied her that unwavering emotion.

The love that was trapped in amber for all time, never to disintegrate.

That never had to be questioned or held onto, so it wouldn't slip away.

When his phone rang, still lost in thought, he picked it up without looking at the screen.

'Theo.' The sound of Nya's brisk voice made his heart start to race. 'I'm sorry to call so early, but can you come and pick up Hope at Carey House?'

'Is there a problem?'

'Hazel just called to let me know she's not feeling well and won't be in today. We have a full schedule, so I have to go in as soon as possible to try to keep everything flowing smoothly.'

'I'll be there in thirty minutes, at the outside.'

'Thank you. I have to run.'

He was already halfway to his bedroom when she hung up, and it took him only a few minutes to change and be on his way.

It turned into one of those days that consisted of putting out one fire after another at the hospital. Theo was glad that, once he got there, he decided to just stay, rather than take Hope back to his house.

'I've asked Lorna to fill in on Reception,' Nya told him, looking totally calm, although the pulse at the base of her neck was thumping. 'But she's totally out of her depth. I'd ask Sophie to keep an eye, but she's off doing home visits, and I need Kiara to see to patients. And I just got a call about a mum who's fallen. A neighbour is bringing her in. I may have to ask you to consult, but then I don't know who will look after Hope.'

'Hey.' He put a hand on her shoulder. 'We'll figure it out.'

She nodded tersely, and went off to supervise her domain.

'Your auntie Nya's not having a good day,' he said to Hope, who kicked her legs in response.

And it got more muddled, as poor Lorna got some files confused, and Nya was trying to sort that out when Carla Nixon—the mum who'd fallen—came in.

Since Lucas Wilde was in with a patient, Nya asked Theo to examine her.

Luckily Hope was napping, and could be

safely left with Lorna for a short time, while Nya came in to assist.

As it turned out, Carla had been alone at home when, on her way to the kitchen, she'd passed out. Luckily her neighbour had come by just after and found her. Frightened for both herself and her baby, she'd called through, and was told to come in.

'Syncope—or fainting—isn't uncommon during pregnancy,' Theo said to the young mother-to-be, before explaining to her about the effects of hormones and increased blood flow coupled with the relaxation of blood vessels. 'I want you to take your time when you stand up, in particular, since that can cause a rush of blood away from the brain.'

Checking her chart, he continued, 'I also want you to make a note of any other instances of dizziness and tell your midwife when next you see her. If there are any other worrying signs, I'm going to make a note on your records that you see your assigned obstetrician.'

After Carla had left, while he was making notes in the computer and Nya was sanitising the room before the next patient, she said, 'You're worried about the possible effects of her syncope?'

'There have been studies that seem to indicate that there may be a correlation between syncope and future medical issues for both mother and baby,' he said. 'While it's not conclusive, and there's no way to know if syncope is a symptom or causation, I always tell patients to advise their practitioners, especially if it happens often. In the past, women have been told it's normal to get light-headed or faint during pregnancy, but I don't subscribe to that way of thinking. Any physical symptoms should be documented.'

'Agreed,' she said, before bustling off again, no doubt to make sure Lorna hadn't set the computer system on fire in her absence.

By the end of the day, Theo could see how tired Nya looked and, taking her aside, he said, 'Listen, you don't have to come by this evening. In fact, why don't you let me keep Hope overnight, so you can get an uninterrupted night's sleep?'

'Don't be silly,' she scoffed. 'I'm fine. Besides, we can't have everyone saying you're turning into Scrooge. Your house is the only one without any decorations visible. It's time to remedy that. I just need a few minutes to speak to Lorna before I can leave.' She gave him a rueful smile, adding, 'I might have been a little abrupt with her today, and want to make sure she knows it wasn't her fault.'

'That's fine,' he said, thinking how wonderfully she managed her staff, making everyone feel comfortable and special. 'There's no rush.'

And as she walked away he once more asked himself if it really was wise to have her over to his house, but was honest enough to admit he didn't care whether it was or not.

He was looking forward to it too much.

CHAPTER ELEVEN

NYA WOKE UP, disorientated and confused.

She was in bed, almost fully clothed—just her shoes missing—but in a room she didn't recognise.

And…

She sat up abruptly.

Where was Hope?

She scrambled to get up, her brain whirring, trying to figure out how she'd slept through the night feedings.

Then it came to her, as she found her shoes neatly placed beside the bed and saw her handbag on the dresser.

She was at Theo's house.

'Oh, Lordy,' she groaned to herself, as she ran her fingers through her hair the best she could, trying to remember what, exactly, had happened the night before.

Theo had insisted on driving her and Hope to his house, stopping on the way to pick up some of The Dolphin Inn's famous fish sandwiches for dinner. Once here, they'd eaten first, and then set about decorating.

Theo had called a halt when Hope had started grizzling for her supper, but when Nya had said, 'I'll get her bottle ready,' Theo had objected.

'Just sit with her, and I'll get it.' He'd given her a cheeky smile, adding, 'I know where everything is.'

'Throwing my words back at me, are you?' she'd asked, putting her nose in the air, even as she'd settled into a corner of his couch, cradling Hope.

'Whenever I get the chance,' he'd called back, from the kitchen.

She'd handed Hope over to him some time thereafter, and recalled doing a teenager-like swoon over just how precious Theo always looked feeding the infant, and then...

Nothing.

Obviously she must have fallen asleep, and he'd carried her to bed.

That thought made her stop with her hand on the doorknob, heat working its way through her torso and up into her face.

Why was it that she regretted not remembering *that* bit of the evening?

She nipped out into the hallway and could

hear Theo's voice in the distance—that sweet, crooning tone he used with Hope—before she went into the bathroom to wash her face.

Ridiculous to feel so nervous, she thought, staring at her reflection for a long moment. It wasn't as though they'd slept together.

Taking a deep breath, berating herself a bit for being silly, she opened the bathroom door and made her way into the living room. Stepping quietly into the doorway, she paused, her heart melting at the sight of Hope lying on a play mat on the floor. Theo was sitting cross-legged beside her, singing softly along with the tune playing on the mobile above her head.

Maybe she made a sound, or he'd been listening for her, but Theo looked up before Nya had a chance to get her emotions under control, and he froze.

Was it her imagination, or did his gaze turn hot for an instant, before it was veiled, and he smiled?

'Good morning.' His voice sounded normal, and he glanced down at Hope, giving Nya a chance to catch an elusive breath. 'I hope we didn't wake you.'

'You definitely didn't,' she said tartly. 'Why'd you let me sleep like that, and make you get up with Hope in the night?'

He shrugged slightly, one finger caught securely in Hope's little fist, his thumb stroking over the back of the infant's hand.

'You were exhausted. There's tea on the hob, or coffee in the cupboard, if you prefer.'

Nya huffed, but his concern for her warmed her straight through, nonetheless.

'At least let me make breakfast.'

Theo laughed, shaking his head. 'If you can find anything in there worth cooking. I told you, I'm rubbish in the kitchen. Why don't you let me take you out for a meal?'

Nya was already looking through the cupboards, and, despite his protestations, had a menu in mind. Clearly when Femi had moved out, she'd left all or most of the tinned goods behind, and there was a loaf of bread in the box, which she determined wasn't too old.

'No need. Breakfast will be ready in a jiff.'

'You must be a miracle worker,' Theo said, his amusement clear.

'I can teach you to cook, if you like,' she replied absently. Then, realising what she'd offered, and how it might sound, added, 'You *can* teach old dogs new tricks.'

'Did you hear what she said to me, Hope? She called me old.'

And having reset the casual, teasing tone

she felt most comfortable with around him, Nya set about making them a meal.

Clearly, with no one to corral his paperwork, Theo had spread it out over the dining table.

'Do you mind if I move some of these things so we can sit here?' she asked, tapping a pile.

'Not at all. There are place mats in the drawer behind you, if you want them.'

Nya shifted a couple of piles of paperwork, but when she picked the third one up, a couple of sheets fell to the floor. Bending, she picked them up and glanced at them, then went still as she realised what they were.

Property sales brochures. One for a house for sale in Luton, another in Chelmsford.

She remembered Theo had spoken about feeling as though he didn't fit in any more, but she hadn't really taken it seriously. In her mind Theo and Carey Cove were synonymous.

Was he really thinking of moving away? Giving up working at both the cottage hospital and St Isolde's too?

She wanted to ask, but the words stuck in her throat. Looking across at him, she allowed herself the luxury of taking him in, fully. Of acknowledging how handsome he was, how much he meant to her, and just how desperately she didn't want him to leave.

Yet hadn't she made the same type of big change when she left Andover and came to Carey Cove? It was impossible not to understand why he might feel the need to go somewhere new, where the past wouldn't keep rearing its head, keeping him in a state of perpetual mourning.

So, instead of bringing it up, she carefully put the brochures back under some other papers and tried to pretend she hadn't seen them.

But although she tried to act normally, the ache around her heart wouldn't go away.

'What are your plans for the day?' Theo asked as they were finishing up breakfast. 'I thought we could go for a drive along the coast, if you'd like.'

Torn, she stared down at her plate for a moment, pretending interest in her last bite of salmon and toast. One part of her wanted to spend as much time with Theo and Hope as possible, knowing this lovely idyll would soon end, but the other part—the wounded heart of her—needed some time alone.

'Although Kiara has been doing so well since she came, I try to stay close to home when she's on call at the hospital, in case she needs me.' That much was true, although Kiara knew she could also call on Sophie, or any of the others if necessary. 'Besides, I have all my usual chores to get done too.'

'Okay,' he said easily, as though it made no difference to him. 'I'll drop you at the clinic to get your car, and probably just come back here with Hope, then.'

No offer to stay and hang about at her cottage, which was how they'd spent the previous Sunday, which, she told herself stoutly, was fine by her. Hadn't she just decided she needed time to get her head around the thought of Theo leaving?

Before she could answer, his phone rang, and he got up to answer it.

From his end of the conversation, she realised he was needed at the hospital, so she quickly gathered up their breakfast things and took them into the kitchen to wash up.

'That was Kiara,' he said, after he hung up. 'Roman's on his way to pick up Molly Chalmers from Scilly. Her husband called to say he was worried about her, and Kiara dispatched the helicopter right away.'

Familiar with Molly, who had type one diabetes, Nya nodded in agreement. 'That was a good call.'

Theo was across the room when he stopped, 'What about Hope?'

'Don't worry,' Nya told him. 'I'll keep her as long as you need.'

He thanked her and rushed off to change. Nya went to where Hope was sleeping in her travel cot, and gently touched her hair, glad not to be going home alone.

Wondering how she was going to manage when they were both gone.

Then she set about collecting Hope's things, and making sure they were ready when Theo was.

Silly as it might be, she felt slightly surreptitious as she got out of his car at the clinic and transferred Hope into hers for the short drive home. It took everything she had not to look around to see if anyone had noticed the transfer, or that she was wearing the same clothing as the day before.

She'd heard about the 'walk of shame' but never thought she, at her age, would ever know what it felt like.

Her mother came by, bringing a tiny multicoloured hat she'd knitted for Hope, using a variation of the floral *aso oke* pattern she'd developed.

'Mum, it's gorgeous!' The rich pinks, purples, and yellow glowed like jewels.

'Hope needs something lovely, and I'm guessing you've been too busy to make her anything.'

'Not true,' Nya said, with feigned annoyance. 'I put your Christmas gift aside to make her a layette set. It's almost finished.'

'Good,' her mother promptly replied. 'Then you'll have time to get mine done before the day.' She sat on the couch and pulled a mask out of her pocket. After putting it on, she held out her arms for the baby.

'She's been a bit grizzly this morning,' Nya warned as she placed Hope in her mother's arms. 'Her nose is still stuffy, but it hasn't got any worse.'

'I'm sure we will be just fine,' Mum replied, with her usual assurance. 'Now, what's happening between you and Theo? I heard you spent the night at his house.'

'Mum.' She felt too raw to talk about it, and tried to infuse a *Stop it now* tone into her voice. 'All that happened was that I fell asleep on his couch.'

But her mother's raised eyebrows spoke of scepticism. 'I'm not suggesting your... involvement with Theodore is a bad thing,' Mum replied at her autocratic best. 'It's time you enjoyed some companionship. But I just thought I should warn you that he may still be on the rebound after his divorce.' When Nya started to reply, her mother's raised hand forestalled her. 'I just don't want to see you hurt, Nya.'

And, in the air between them, she heard the word 'again', although her mother hadn't said it.

Later that morning, after Mum had left, Theo called to say he was transferring Molly to St Isolde's by ambulance.

'I don't like how uncontrollable her diabetes has become,' he told Nya. 'And I've given the doctors there my opinion that they should do a caesarean as soon as possible.'

Surprised, Nya asked, 'You're not going with her?'

'No.' There was a bit of terseness in his tone, but then it softened. 'My locum is on hand, and I'll leave it to him. As soon as I'm squared away here, I'll come and get Hope.'

'Okay, but just a warning, she's been fussy all morning.'

'She is all right?'

'I think so,' Nya replied. 'No fever, and I haven't had to suction. Sometimes babies just want a bit more cuddling than usual.'

'She'll certainly get all she needs from me,' he said, in that fond, loving tone he so often used when talking about Hope. Then she heard him blow out a breath, and say, 'Hey, if you're not too busy, can we still go for that drive along the coast? I feel like getting out for a bit, and I'd love the company.'

Silly heart, to do that little stutter step, and Nya knew she should refuse, but in his voice she heard his continued annoyance at being sidelined at St Isolde's, even if it were for his own good.

And she found herself saying, 'Sure. I'll dress Hope warmly, since it looks like rain.'

The truth was, Theo didn't want to go home without Nya, even with Hope.

The night before, when he'd looked up and realised she'd fallen asleep curled up on his couch, the wave of need that swept him had rocked him back on his heels.

With her face softened with sleep, those all too knowing eyes veiled, she'd looked as soft and tender as the infant in his arms. Yet, there was no ignoring the lush curves and generous mouth that he longed to explore again.

He'd been reluctant to pick her up and carry her to bed, because he just knew that holding her that way would be torment. And it had been—sweet torment, and almost overwhelming temptation.

Nya had hardly stirred, just murmured

under her breath as he'd picked her up, and snuggled her face into his neck, causing a cascade of gooseflesh over his skin.

Oh, how he'd wanted her just then.

And when he'd put her on the bed in the guest room, he'd stood looking down at her for a long moment, trying to work through the complex emotions battering him.

There'd been no answers forthcoming, and he'd swiftly removed her shoes, then left the room before he gave in to the desire to simply lie down beside her and pull her close.

Going back into the living room, he'd pulled up some of the house listings he'd saved on his computer and begun going through them again. He'd been playing with the idea of leaving Carey Cove for months, and now he knew doing so would be the right thing.

If being with Nya and Hope for one week could unsettle him this way, make him care so much, what would happen to him when it was all over?

When Carey Cove once more went from being a homey haven to a place of tormented memories?

Yet, there was a part of him that was determined to enjoy this found family as long as he could. And perhaps, in spending time with

Nya, he would figure out that it wasn't the big emotional deal he was making it out to be.

He went to pick them up and couldn't help laughing in appreciation when he saw Hope's jaunty new hat.

'Iona's been hard at work, I see,' he said, and got a grin from Nya.

'Oh, you know her so well.'

He drove down towards Land's End, planning to circle around and back to Penzance for an early tea.

There was something a bit different in Nya's mood, but it didn't make the day less enjoyable. In fact, she seemed more relaxed than she'd been that morning.

Which was surprising, once she said, 'I have to warn you: it's already being spread around the village that I spent the night at yours last night.'

Thankful that they'd stopped for dinner and he wasn't driving, he watched her face as he asked, 'How did you hear that?'

She snorted. 'Mum. When she came by this morning.'

'What do you want to do about this?'

Nya shrugged. 'Nothing. If anyone asks me, I'll tell the truth—that I fell asleep on your couch. It's not that big a deal, and no one's business, to boot.'

'It looks like, between us, Hope and I are ruining your stellar reputation,' he joked, only to have her turn those dark, somehow shadowed eyes his way.

And although she was smiling, he didn't believe her light-hearted tone when she replied, 'It's about time, don't you think? After all, all work and no play make for a dull life, right? And who wants to be known as boring?'

What on earth could he say to that?

'Anyone who calls you dull is an idiot,' he said, shaking his head.

She wrinkled her nose, rocking Hope back and forth against her bosom. 'I know myself, Theo. I work, knit, do a little gardening, volunteer occasionally. I haven't travelled much, or done anything exciting, and have no interest in going outside my comfort zone, really. If that's not the definition of boring, I don't know what is.'

It didn't sound boring to him, and he said so.

'We live in a time when everything is online and visible—faraway places, exciting adventures, every material thing you can imagine. So many people get sucked into wanting more and more, often at the cost of their peace of mind.'

He stopped, wondering if somewhere along the line his ex-wife hadn't got sucked into that very trap. Then he mentally shrugged the thought away. Femi was no longer any of his concern.

'Contentment is difficult for most people to find,' he went on, smiling across at Nya, who had gone still, and was watching him with an intensity that held his gaze on hers. 'You've somehow found that—found a life that I think you've been happy living. There's nothing truly boring about that, is there?'

Her eyelids drooped, so he could no longer see the expression in her eyes, and just then the waiter came to ask if there was anything else they needed, and they somehow never resumed the conversation.

Leaving Theo wondering if she agreed with his assessment or not.

CHAPTER TWELVE

THEO THOUGHT SHE was content and comfortable.

If anyone had said that just a week or so ago, she might even have happily agreed, but today she felt neither of those emotions.

Instead, she felt restless and needy, and discontented with everything.

She'd thought she'd come to terms with all the things in life she'd never have, yet in Theo and Hope's company her prior choices—and loss—were more painful.

Coming to terms with never being a mother, or having someone who loved her the way Jim would have, had been hard. At some point she'd thought she had, but now she was forced to admit that dream hadn't really died.

Or maybe you had to actually hold something in your hands, feel the emotional heartbeat of it, to *really* know what you were missing.

Sitting across the table from Theo, with Hope a sweet weight against her chest, Nya knew *this* was what she wanted.

What she *craved*.

What she would only have for a short—far too short—time.

Family, in all its incarnations.

Soul-soothing companionship.

Love shared, without restriction.

But none of that was meant to be—at least not for much longer—and so she swallowed the bitter sense of lost time and forlorn dreams, putting it all aside. Not wanting Theo to sense her disquiet.

From somewhere deep inside, from the place where all her fears and pain lived, she found the strength she needed to make small talk with him while they drove back towards Carey Cove. It was moments like this, as she sensed the day coming to an end, that she longed, more than ever, to extend their time together.

When she looked back on this period of having this unusual little family, she wanted as many wonderful memories as she could hold in her mind.

Dusk was falling as they drove back into

Carey Cove, and Nya leaned her head back against the seat, watching the final rays of the sun touching the western sky. As they went over the little hill outside the village, Carey House came into view, and Nya sat up.

'What on earth…?'

The parking area was full, and an ambulance stood outside the patient entrance, making Nya wonder if it was there to collect a patient, or drop one off.

'That doesn't look good, does it?'

Theo slowed the car as he spoke, and Nya leaned forward so as to see better.

'No, it doesn't. It looks as though Hazel's still there too, and she should have gone home ages ago.'

The car picked up speed again, continuing down the road towards the hospital entrance. Sophie was in charge today, and probably had everything under control, but even so Nya couldn't help worrying.

'Theo, do you mind—?'

Before she'd even finished, Theo had turned on the indicator, and was slowing to make the turn into the hospital driveway.

'How did you know what I was going to ask?' When she glanced at him, he was smiling in that sly, sexy way he had. 'I thought you'd have just kept going.'

'Just so you could spend the rest of the evening stewing and wondering what was going on here?' he asked as he found a spot to park. 'Or jump on the phone before we even got home?'

Even as worried as she was, Nya couldn't help laughing as she reached for the door handle.

'When did you get to know me this well?'

Theo didn't reply to her question, but said, 'Go on in. I'll bring Hope.'

How like him to be so understanding, Nya thought as she hurried into the reception area.

Hazel looked up almost fearfully when she heard the door open.

'Oh, thank goodness,' the receptionist said on recognising Nya. 'I thought it was another patient coming in. Did Sophie call you?'

'No,' Nya replied. 'I was passing by and saw all the vehicles. What's going on?'

'Five expectant mothers turned up, one after another, over the last fifteen minutes. One came by ambulance from St Buryan, where she was on holiday. Then Margie Landry, Velma Jones, and Karin Howell came in, one after the other.'

The latter three women were all mums-to-be who Nya knew were due or overdue, so she wasn't terribly surprised, except for the fact they all decided to go into labour at the same time!

'And the fifth?'

Hazel lowered her voice, although it was just the two of them in the room.

'Tara Mitchell-Powers. Avis's daughter. She's not due for another month, but Avis is convinced she's in labour, so she brought her in.'

Just then the door opened, and Theo came in—baby Hope's carry seat in one hand, holding the door with the other, his phone tucked between shoulder and chin. For a moment Nya froze, thrown back in time to the day he'd first found Hope on the doorstep, and Nya had first felt that surge of attraction towards him.

Was it really only days ago, although it felt as if a lifetime had passed?

'I'm actually just stepping into the hospital now, Avis. Yes, I'll come right up.'

Nya pulled herself together to ask, 'Avis called you about Tara?'

'Yes. I've never heard her in such a state.' Everyone knew Avis Mitchell was the quintessential unflappable, no-nonsense type. 'She said she wouldn't feel comfortable unless I examined Tara.'

'Well, it's her only child, and first grand-child. I'm not surprised.'

Theo nodded. 'Me neither. Do you mind taking care of Hope for a while?'

He was talking to Nya, but Hazel jumped in before she could answer.

'I don't mind at all.'

Nya gave the receptionist a laughing look. 'It's way past time for you to be going home. Artie will wonder where you are and send out a search party.'

'I already told him I was staying late,' Hazel replied, taking the seat out of Theo's hand. 'And I'm sure Dr Theo would be happy for your help, since it's all hands on deck up there.'

Still chuckling, Nya gave in, and followed Theo to the stairs, explaining what was happening to him as they made their way to the labour ward.

Once there, Nya paused, and took in the sight of more relatives and friends than they were used to having to accommodate. The entire waiting room was filled to capacity. Standing room only.

As soon as Avis saw them, she came rushing towards them.

'Oh, Theo. I'm so glad you're here.' Avis

pretty much collapsed into his arms. 'I don't trust anyone but you.'

'There, there.' Theo patted Avis on the back, his expression solicitous—his tone calming. 'You stay here while I examine Tara, so we can see what's going on.'

As he walked towards the nurses' station, Nya at his side, Sophie came out of one of the labour rooms, and her face lit up when she saw them.

Coming close, she whispered, 'Thank goodness you're both here. We're stretched to breaking, and Avis has been having a conniption. When she told me she was going to call Dr Turner, I'm afraid I was a little sharp with her—saying she should go ahead, although her daughter is having Braxton Hicks contractions and seems in perfectly good nick.'

'Avis has a lot on her plate just now,' Nya told the younger woman gently, but she also gave Sophie's arm a commiserating squeeze. She knew only too well how frustrating it could be in their line of work. 'How are the other mums doing?'

Theo had gone to wash up, while Sophie gave Nya a quick rundown.

'Velma Jones just delivered. Baby and mum doing perfectly well. Margie Landry's labour isn't progressing quickly, but baby isn't in any distress, and Karin Howell is at seven centimetres dilation. It's the visitor that came in by ambulance I'm most worried about.'

Nya took the chart Sophie held out to her, and read the notes, as Sophie continued, 'Brittney Henderson, thirty-three, second child, only thirty-six weeks along, no history of premature labour. She was visiting relatives when she started having what she thought were Braxton Hicks contractions. When she noticed some spotting, her aunt called for an ambulance, since she didn't want to take any chances.'

'Good for her,' Nya said, absently, still reading Sophie's notes. The patient's contractions were seven minutes apart, and the ultrasound had shown the baby was transverse.

'If Theo has a chance after he checks on Tara, I'd appreciate him taking a look at Mrs Henderson. I was going to wait a bit more before calling in the consulting obstetrician on duty, but, since he's here, I want his opinion on whether I should send her on to St Isolde's. I asked the ambulance to wait, and they agreed, unless they're needed elsewhere.'

'I'll let him know,' Nya said, realising she might have to rescue Theo from Avis. 'Let me go and see how he's getting on.'

After scrubbing her hands thoroughly, she made her way to the room Tara had been put in. Opening the door, she realised that Theo had obviously done what Sophie hadn't managed.

He'd calmed Avis down.

'So, I think the best thing is to go back to your mum and dad's and get some rest. If the contractions start again, move around—change position—and see if they go away. If you have any other symptoms, come back to Carey House.'

'You're sure she isn't in labour? She's been so stressed about Don, and travelled all the way from Milton Keynes…'

Well, perhaps not all the way calmed, although while Avis asked the question she was helping her daughter put on her shoes, obviously in preparation to leave.

'Oh, Mum,' Tara sighed, sounding more exasperated than worried. 'If Dr Turner says I'm fine, I believe him. You've always said what a wonderful doctor he is. Even asked me if I didn't want to come down here so he would be on hand in case there were any problems when I delivered.'

'I know. I know.' Avis gave both Theo and Nya wan smiles as Tara's silent husband helped his wife up off the bed. 'First grand-baby and all that, I suppose.'

'Totally understandable,' Theo said, with a smile, as they made their way out into the corridor. 'Take care, now.'

Then he looked down at Nya, and said, 'I just need to write up these notes, and then we can go.'

'Actually, Sophie was hoping you'd give her your opinion on another patient before you go. Brittney Henderson, a visitor that was brought in by ambulance. Sophie has the ambulance waiting, in case you think they should transport her on to St Isolde's.'

For the first time since she'd known him, Theo seemed to hesitate when asked for his professional input, but then he nodded, and said, 'Let me look at the file.'

That momentary pause, that expression of near annoyance, made Nya wonder what he was thinking, but before she could ask Theo was striding towards the nurses' station.

Theo tamped down the surprising spurt of ir-ritation he'd felt as he wrote up the few notes on Tara's card. Nya waited patiently beside him, the chart for the patient she wanted him to see in hand.

Rather than stay at the hospital any longer,

what he really wanted to do was take Nya and Hope home.

Help to feed and bathe the baby, then snuggle with her as Nya's gentle voice read Hope a story, and the infant nodded off to sleep in his arms.

There was, in his mind, this constant *tick-tick-tick* of the time they'd have together slipping away, and he didn't want to miss a moment.

Yet, with all that was happening at Carey House, his conscience and professional pride wouldn't let him leave.

Taking the chart from Nya's hand, cognisant of how late it was getting, he reluctantly said, 'If you want to take Hope home, I can give you my keys. I can walk to your cottage when I'm finished here.'

Nya's smile did funny things to his insides. Made his heart skip a beat, and his stomach muscles tighten.

'Let's see what your opinion of the patient is before I go and try to pry Hope away from Hazel. She's already called her husband to tell him she'll be late home, so I don't think she's in a huge rush just yet.'

Just then, Sophie came over and announced, 'Karin's just about nine centimetres now, so

I'm going back in to deliver her baby. Have you seen Mrs Henderson yet?'

'Just heading in there now,' Theo replied, his gaze on the file in his hand. 'Premature labour, thirty-six weeks... Did anyone come in with her?'

'Her aunt, who she was staying with.'

No dad in sight yet, then. Theo didn't ask any further questions, but was aware of Nya trailing after him as he set off for her room.

Brittney Henderson turned a narrow-eyed gaze their way as they entered, and the older woman sitting at her bedside straightened to add her own suspicious glare.

'Mrs Henderson, my name is Dr Theo Turner, and this is Head Midwife Nya Ademi. Midwife French asked me to examine you and determine what the best course of treatment should be.'

'She said I was in premature labour,' Mrs Henderson said, her tone as hard as her expression. But Theo noticed the gleam of tears in her eyes and wondered if it was the stress of her present situation alone making her want to cry. 'Does that mean the baby's coming now?'

'It may be, but I'd like to run a couple more tests to see exactly how far along you are.' Turning to the aunt, who was silently watching the exchange, he added, 'If you don't mind giving us some privacy for a few minutes?'

As Nya prepared the ultrasound machine, Theo tried to gently coax some additional information out of his patient. And, as it turned out, she was staying with her aunt because she'd had a massive row with her husband back in Norwich and decided to leave.

'I told him I wouldn't stand for his nonsense,' she said stoutly, but despite her best efforts her voice wavered just a little. 'So while he was at work, I took my son and came away to Aunt Ruth's. I never thought there'd be any problem for the baby.'

'Don't blame yourself,' Nya said softly. 'Babies come when they're ready, whether we are, or not.'

No mention of how stress and travelling at such a late stage in pregnancy could induce premature labour. Just comforting words and that gentle manner. Not that Theo would expect anything less. Nya was a born caretaker, with a huge heart and overwhelming compassion.

Just then she looked up and their gazes met, creating a cascade of emotions Theo wasn't sure how to categorise. All he knew was that being the focus of her regard just then, even for the brief moment before she turned back to their patient, filled him with warmth and longing.

And a visceral fear that he'd lost himself—his heart—at a time, and in a way, he could least afford, and didn't know how to deal with, at all.

CHAPTER THIRTEEN

LATER THAT NIGHT Nya lay in bed staring at the ceiling, thinking back on the day just gone and trying to relax enough to go to sleep.

Theo had administered drugs both to promote the development of the baby's lungs and slow Brittney Henderson's contractions, then sent her by ambulance to St Isolde's.

'Hopefully they won't have to do a caesarean section,' he'd told the patient as he'd carefully explained what he was doing. 'But do prepare yourself for the possibility.'

Nya had offered to call her husband, but after some consideration, Brittney had said she'd do it herself.

'Better I tell him,' she'd said, damp-eyed again. 'If he hears it from anyone else, it'll just make things worse.'

As it turned out, the Hendersons' argument hadn't been about anything important.

'Jamie says I've been a bit crazed this time

around, and he's right,' Brittney had admitted. 'I don't remember being this emotional with my first. Or as stroppy.'

'Just like each baby is different, each pregnancy is too,' Theo had reassured her, and Nya had agreed.

'On top of the variance in hormones, there are all the external factors too. Changes in your home life, any financial difficulties that didn't exist when you were expecting your first can make a big difference too.'

Thus reassured, Brittney had been put back into the ambulance, and sent on to Falmouth.

Theo had written up his notes, and they'd collected Hope from Hazel, bringing her home just in time for her early evening feed.

Theo had stayed, helping Nya get Hope ready for bed as he so often did. Being next to him at the sink, hearing his every breath, feeling his warmth against her arm, inhaling his scent, had made the sensation of disgruntlement she'd experienced earlier return.

Why, she wondered, did life insist on giving her a taste of paradise, and then yanking it away? Giving her this brief, wonderful time with a man and a child, neither of whom would ever be hers?

Yet more of her mother's words of five years ago came back to her, reminding her she'd made a choice not to move on from Jim's death.

'You've closed yourself off from life. From the opportunity to build a life with someone, have children of your own. One day you're going to look back and wonder what you were thinking, and why you let the chance of happiness pass you by.'

Nya had been angry and hurt. Didn't Mum understand that losing Jim had meant giving all of that up, anyway? That for her own peace, she'd locked all of those urges away, and got on with her life as best she could?

Jim had been her soulmate. The one person who had made her feel truly alive in every sense.

His exuberance had been contagious. Growing up, she'd been solemn, studious, conscientious, because that was what she'd needed to be, especially after her father died.

Dad's death had left her floundering, all too aware of how capricious life could be, and when she'd met Jim, and he'd tried to sweep her off her feet, she'd resisted as long as she could.

How could she get involved with a man with such a dangerous job?

But Jim had got under her skin, and into her heart, and she'd lulled herself into believing nothing would go wrong. He'd made it easy to believe too.

'Safe as houses,' he'd said. 'If it wasn't, there wouldn't be so many old army veterans about, would there?'

Then he'd laughed that rich, booming laugh, and she'd just melted.

James Ademi could have made her believe anything, risk anything, give everything.

And she had—to her detriment.

When he'd died, he'd taken all her trust, her hopes with him, and left her nothing but fear, and the overriding knowledge that she didn't dare risk loving again.

What she'd told Theo, about thinking she'd eventually leave Carey Cove and look for a more fulfilling life somewhere else had, she thought now, been a big fat fib.

She'd always been too afraid, even though she'd refused to admit it, even to herself.

Now, she had to face that fact, and acknowledge she was still too afraid to reach for what she now knew she wanted.

Theo, and Hope, for ever.

Oh, she knew Hope was just with her for a little while, and while that was heartbreaking in itself, she could bear it—just. All she wanted, in the final analysis, was for Hope to have the very best life possible, hopefully with her mother or father or, if that wasn't possible, with a wonderful family who'd raise her as their own.

But Theo? Theo was still hurting from his divorce, still trying to figure out how to move on, and once again Mum had hit the nail on the head.

If Nya let him know that she was interested in him, physically and emotionally, and it turned out to just be a rebound situation on his part, she'd be devastated again.

She wasn't the quickie affair type—that much she knew for sure.

And she couldn't risk wanting more.

Flopping over in bed, hugging a pillow, she considered her options.

In a week, the midwife hired to cover Marnie's maternity leave would be arriving, and, although it would stretch the team even further than they already were, Nya would take leave. Then she could tell Theo she would take over Hope's care on her own, limiting the amount of time they spent together.

Then, with a sigh, she realised that plan wouldn't work.

Theo was committed to Hope's care, and he was a man who never walked away from responsibility. Even telling him she didn't need his help wouldn't stop him from helping anyway.

And the change being around Hope had wrought in Theo was too wonderful for Nya to risk interfering with it. He was smiling again. Seemed more alive—less solemn and sad. He needed Hope even more than the infant needed him.

No.

Nya would just have to deal with the emotional turmoil she'd brought on herself as best she could, until the situation resolved itself.

Until Hope was relocated.

Until Theo left Carey Cove and moved on with his life.

And she could go back to her safe, boring existence.

She'd left the Christmas lights on in the living room, and the colourful flashes of light illuminated the room enough to allow her to see Jim's picture. His glorious smile. The strong arms that had made her feel safe and treasured.

In a way, she thought she'd let him down. He'd had a zest for life, and an indefatigable spirit that had made each day with him a delight. If she'd wanted to honour his memory properly, she should have taken up skydiving, or rock climbing. Moved to the South Seas and become a pearl diver.

Instead, she'd run away from life.

And, as she finally fell asleep, she was wondering whether she'd ever feel content with her life again.

There was no way to know how long she'd slept when she suddenly jerked awake and, without knowing why, immediately sat up.

A quick glance at her clock showed it was just gone midnight and, as she swung her legs out of bed, searching with her toes for her slippers, she was listening intently. Had someone been trying to break in?

Then, she heard it, and rushed to turn on the light.

Hope's breathing sounded wrong.

Laboured.

The cot was right beside the bed, and Nya was there, looking down at Hope in an instant.

The baby's chest was heaving and, as Nya watched, it stopped moving altogether.

Was that a blue tinge around her lips, too?

Quickly snatching her up with shaking hands, Nya ran for her phone.

Theo was still awake, poring over property listings, when his phone rang, making his heart skip a beat.

Calls after midnight were never a good thing.

And when he saw Nya's name on the screen, his heart rate went into gallop mode.

'Nya?'

'Hope's not breathing properly.' Her voice was shaky, uneven, and Theo was on his feet, already heading for the door, as she continued. 'I've already called an ambulance.'

'I'm on my way,' he said, snatching up his car keys and medical bag. 'What are her symptoms?'

Nya outlined them quickly, her voice getting steadier, probably because now it was medical jargon, and her training was kicking in.

'I just don't understand. She's been a little off colour the last couple of days, with that slightly stuffy nose and being a bit fussy, but I've not noticed any other symptoms. How could this come on so quickly?'

He was in his car and put the phone on speaker as he started it up. 'I didn't notice anything either, Nya.' He was already kicking himself for that, but didn't want her beating herself up. 'We don't know what's happening, so don't start blaming yourself.'

It took only minutes for him to get to Nya's, and she was right there to open the door for him. Her drawn, grey-hued face made his heart clench, and his chest tightened when he saw Hope, limp in Nya's arms, her chest heaving with each breath.

'She's getting worse,' Nya said. 'Where do you want to examine her?'

'On the couch,' he said, setting down his medical bag and taking out his stethoscope. 'What's the ETA on the ambulance?'

She glanced at her watch. 'About five minutes, I think.'

He listened to Hope's chest, worried not just by the obvious pulmonary obstruction, but by the infant's lethargy.

'Get a bag ready for her,' he said, keeping his voice level with effort, wanting to give Nya something to concentrate on. 'And put on your clothes. If you go with her in the ambulance, I'll follow in my car.'

He heard her breath hitch, and then she rushed off towards her room, leaving him and Hope alone in the living room.

Hope's face scrunched, as though she wanted to cry, but she didn't seem to have the strength.

'Come on,' he muttered, as though the ambulance driver could hear him telepathically. 'Come on.'

The swift onset of the infant's symptoms worried him.

Asthma? Bacterial or viral infection? Allergy?

As a doctor, all these questions were instinctive, but Theo really was only focused on Hope's breathing. He found himself inhaling, as if trying to give her more air by osmosis—the actions of a father, rather than a medical practitioner.

He was so glad Nya had called an ambulance. Right now, he was going on adrenaline, but he knew he wasn't fit to drive safely if he had to take Hope to Falmouth, and there was no time to call out Roman and the helicopter.

'Come on. Come *on*.'

Hope's cyanosis was getting worse.

He heard the sirens in the distance, and the rush of relief almost brought him to his knees. Nya came dashing out of her room, Hope's baby bag over her shoulder and a tote in her other hand, which she tossed down near the door.

She seemed to have got a better grip on her emotions, since her voice was steady when she said, 'Bring that bag with you when you come, please. I'll be staying with Hope for as long as necessary. I'll call Kiara when we get to Falmouth, and the paediatrician has looked at our baby.'

Flashing lights heralded the arrival of the ambulance, and Nya pulled the door open before the attendants were even out of the vehicle.

How many times had he put a patient into an ambulance and, although concerned, hadn't felt as though his entire world were shattered by it? Too many to count, really. But this time, as he stumbled over his words, telling the ambulance attendants what he'd observed, it took everything he had to let Hope go.

With brisk efficiency, Hope was taken to the ambulance and Nya paused only long enough to thrust her house keys into Theo's hand before she followed.

Then, siren going, the vehicle pulled away, leaving Theo standing in the driveway, watching it, until it disappeared.

'Theo!' The urgency of the voice coming from behind him had him spinning around. 'Theo, what happened? Is it Nya? Hope?'

Iona, in a dressing gown and winter boots, her head wrapped in a silk scarf, her eyes wide and her voice frantic, came running towards him.

'It's Hope. She's developed a problem with her lungs.'

He tried to sound matter-of-fact, but the desperation he felt couldn't be masked, and the next thing he knew Iona was hugging him, tightly.

'She'll be all right, Theo. Keep the faith.'

Then she held his shoulders, and stepped back, so she was looking up into his face.

'Let me pack Nya a bag, and then you have to pull yourself together and go after them. They'll need you.'

'Yes,' he said. 'Yes.' But he remained rooted where he was, until Iona gave his shoulders a hard shake.

'Now, Theodore. Come on.'

That autocratic voice jerked him out of the shaking stupor he'd fallen into, and he snapped into action, following Iona into the house.

'Nya packed that tote,' he said.

'Poor baby.' Iona was giving it a go-through, and seemed to find the contents inadequate. 'Give me a moment.'

In what seemed like an age, but couldn't have been more than five minutes, he was in his car with Nya's repacked tote, plus another bag Iona tossed onto the back seat.

'Her knitting,' she said as she leaned in to

kiss Theo's cheek. 'She'll need something to do with her hands. I'll lock up. And make sure you keep your mind on the road, Theo. There'll be time enough for worrying when you get there.'

But it was only as he was driving away, trying his best to keep within the speed limit, that Nya's words came back to him, and struck him like a blow to the chest...

Our baby.

And he had to blink against the tears that threatened to fill his eyes.

CHAPTER FOURTEEN

THE NEXT THREE days were some of the longest of Nya's life, and she didn't know how she would have got through them without Theo's calm strength.

'Severe bronchiolitis,' the paediatrician diagnosed. 'Without a history, it's difficult to say exactly why she was so susceptible, or why it presented with such rapid onset. Right now, we're making sure she remains oxygenated and hydrated.' He hesitated for a moment, glancing from Nya to Theo, then back again, before continuing, 'We're monitoring her oxygen levels and lung function carefully. Hopefully we won't have to intubate.'

It was only when she felt Theo's arm around her waist that Nya realised she'd sagged at the knees, joints made watery by the thought of just how very ill Hope was.

The hospital staff had Hope in a special cot, where she could receive humidified oxygen and a saline drip. It had taken everything Nya had inside not to cry the first time she was allowed into the room and saw Hope with the tubes and monitors attached to her tiny frame.

'It looks worse than it is, Mum,' the nurse said, patting Nya's arm.

How many times had she said something similar to a patient over all the years she'd worked as a nurse, without understanding just how devastating seeing a child that way was? Oh, she knew, intellectually, but now she was experiencing it with her heart, and it was almost too much to bear.

As she sat in the chair the nurse put for her next to Hope's cot, all Nya could do was stare at the baby, noting her pallor, the still laboured breathing. Occasionally glancing at the monitors to check her oxygen levels, heart rate and blood pressure, praying, *bargaining* for them to improve—willing Hope to get better.

Mum came each day, to offer her support and bring both Nya and Theo food. And the day after Hope had been admitted, Hazel had shown up during evening visiting hours. When Nya had hugged her, and thanked her for coming, the receptionist had burst into tears.

'You don't think she caught that virus from me, do you?' she'd sobbed, clinging to Nya. 'I would have never offered to take care of Hope if I knew I'd be exposing her to a virus.'

'I'm sure you didn't make her sick, Hazel. Viruses, like the one they think Hope has, take up to two weeks to incubate, so she was probably already infected when she came to us.'

Hazel's relief had been palpable, but neither that nor her misplaced guilt had truly penetrated Nya's mental fog.

It took everything she had just to put one foot in front of the other. Everything inside her was focused on Hope, and each precious breath the baby took.

But she understood Hazel's guilt. Only too well. She'd known that a baby less than a month old, with an unknown history, should be protected. Now, she knew she hadn't done enough. That she'd possibly made things worse by her lack of care—exposing Hope to the clinic and a variety of people. Taking her out and about, when they should have kept her indoors.

Well, she was paying the price now, wasn't she?

She didn't need to look up to know when Theo came into the nursery. Somehow, over the last few days, she'd developed a type of radar attuned just to him. So, when he sat down beside her and reached for her hand, all she felt was relief as she curled her fingers around his.

'Your turn,' he said quietly, but with that hint of steel in his tone. 'Go and get something to eat.'

'I'm really not hungry.'

'Then at least go and walk around for a little. Get some fresh air. You'll be of no use to Hope if you collapse from hunger and exhaustion.'

They'd been allowed to stay past visiting hours for the last two nights, returning to Theo's Falmouth flat for a little while. Then, as soon as was feasible, they'd returned to the hospital to keep vigil.

Nya knew Theo was suffering too. It was there in his eyes, and in the deepening lines bracketing his mouth and creasing his forehead. There was also the fact that, as she lay in the guest bedroom at his flat, fitfully dozing, she could hear him quietly pacing back and forth in the living area. Knowing he too was unable to sleep through worry increased her own tension. That was the only other thing Nya felt—the need to make sure he was okay.

It was strange to have someone to support and be supported by. Yet, whenever she thought of getting up and joining him, she hesitated. The only things he asked of her was that she stay fed and hydrated and get some rest. If he knew she wasn't sleeping, he'd worry even more.

And now, not wanting to increase his stress levels, she gave in.

'I have my phone,' she said as she got up. 'Call me if there's any change.'

Theo had stood up too, and he squeezed Nya's fingers, tugging gently at her hand until she looked up at him.

'I will. Keep the faith, Nya. She'll get through this. *We'll* get through it.'

From what felt like the depths of her belly she dredged up a smile, although she knew it was a weak effort at best.

'Yes.'

But after she walked away what stayed with her, along with the fear of losing Hope, was the thought that his statement that they'd get through it was untrue.

In the final analysis there was no 'we'.

They were united now through their separate love of Hope, but once she was no longer in their lives, whatever this union between them was would also dissolve. Theo would be moving on, hopefully to build a good new life for himself.

And just now Nya couldn't help being glad. Even if Hope pulled through, the entire situation had reiterated how fragile life was, and how much it hurt to think of losing someone else she loved...

Loved?

She meant Hope, right? Just Hope.

Her brain shied away from the thought that it was more than that.

There was too much on her plate right now to consider otherwise.

As Nya left the nursery Theo sank back into his chair and, being alone with the baby, allowed himself to rub his hands over his face, weariness weighing him down.

He was trying so hard to keep it all together for Nya, but inside he was falling apart, bit by bit, each day that Hope didn't improve.

Nya seemed to think, because he was a father, this was a situation he'd been in before—or that these were emotions he'd already experienced. But his son and daughter had been healthy children. The worst he, as a parent, had experienced was when Gillian broke her collarbone at eleven.

But this—watching Hope struggle to breathe, not even having the energy to cry properly when they suctioned her nasal passages—was something far different.

Heartbreaking.

Terrifying.

And seeing Nya struggle, that shell-shocked expression in her eyes, was even more devastating.

He couldn't recall a time when he'd felt more powerless.

Theo looked up at the light tap on the glass to see Iona outside looking in at him. With a jerk of her chin, she let it be known that she wanted to speak to him and, since the hospital was only letting Nya and him into the nursery, he got up to go and speak to her.

'Will you be in the room for a while?' he asked the nurse, who was checking Hope's lines and nappy. 'I shouldn't be gone long.'

'I'll be here until you get back, Dr Turner. Take your time.'

As Theo closed the nursery door behind himself, it came to him that Iona looked as if she had aged ten years over the last few days. There were stress lines at the corners of her eyes, and the skin of her face above her mask had lost its lustre, making it seem dull and pale.

'How is Hope?' she asked.

'Still the same.' He couldn't tell her that the doctors were taking about intubating—the words sticking in his throat.

'Oh, Theo.' Iona's eyes glistened, and he knew she was holding back tears. 'Isn't there any medication they can give her? Something more they can do to help?'

'They're doing all that they can, Iona.'

He said it gently, even though he wanted to shout. Ask if she didn't think he was monitoring Hope himself, making sure everything possible was being done. But he knew Iona was just as concerned as he and Nya were.

'Where is Nya?'

'I sent her to get something to eat, although I'm not sure she'll take my advice.'

Iona lifted her glasses and rubbed her eyes.

'Nya tends to retreat into herself when she's sad, or frightened.' Iona sighed and settled her glasses back in place. 'And she's had so much loss in her life, I can only imagine what's going on in her head.' She was staring straight into Theo's eyes, when she continued, 'I'm glad you're here, with her. You'll keep her from shutting down completely.'

Would he, though?

It felt as though, in this too, he was failing.

Nya was there, physically, but she had, as

her mother said, retreated to the point where Theo felt there was an emotional chasm between them. When he reached out to her, trying to impart what strength he had to offer, there was no sign that she recognised or accepted it.

Once more he was left impotent to make things right—for Hope, or for Nya—and that failure cut him to the depths of his soul.

'Theo,' Iona said. 'Don't give up on her because she seems unreachable. All I ask is that you see her through whatever happens, as best you can.'

Before he could reply, he heard Nya's distinctive footsteps approaching, and he turned to watch her walk towards them.

How stiffly she held herself, as though relaxing even a little would cause her to fall apart. Seeing her like that made him want to take her in his arms and hold her close. Give her everything and anything he had, so as to make it all better, even though he knew it wouldn't really help.

'Mum. What're you doing here so late? Did you drive all the way from Carey Cove?'

'No, love.' Iona leaned forward and, holding her daughter's shoulders, pressed her cheek against Nya's. 'I've been staying in

Penzance, to be a little closer. Have you eaten? Got any rest today?'

Nya looked as though she didn't know what those words meant, and she shook her head.

'I'm fine, Mum. I just took a little walk and got a cup of tea.'

Iona's chin came up, and she gave her daughter a stern look.

'Nya, you look dead on your feet. Go with Theo. Have some dinner and get some rest. You have to take care of yourself.'

'That's what Theo's been saying,' she replied, almost absently. 'But how can I leave her?'

'She's in the best of hands. You running yourself into the ground isn't going to help her. It's almost the end of visiting hours, so go. I'm sure they'll call you immediately, if there's any change.'

Theo found himself holding his breath, and when Nya looked at him, all he could do was nod, silently willing her to let him in, and let him take care of her.

Nya took a deep, shuddering breath and, as she released it, she nodded.

'Okay.'

Theo let out the breath he'd been holding.

'I'll tell the nurses what we're doing, and meet you downstairs,' he said, wanting Iona to walk Nya out, so she didn't have a chance to change her mind.

'Agreed,' Iona said briskly. 'Come, Nya.'

Now, at least, there was a plan to follow—some action to take.

Get Nya to eat, to get some rest.

Somehow, in some small way, help her relax.

He'd order some food and pick it up on the way home. Instead of sitting at the dining table, he'd turn on the gas fire and they'd eat in the living room, casually and comfortably.

Going downstairs, he found Nya and Iona in the lobby of the hospital. Outside, the grey, rainy day had morphed into a cool, damp, windy night. As he approached the two women, he saw the way Nya twisted the straps of her knitting bag between her fingers in a physical manifestation of her restless agony of spirit.

She'd carried the bag back and forth from the flat to the hospital, but rarely took her needlework out. There was a disconnected air about her, which now made sense in light of Iona's explanation of how Nya reacted to emotional pain by retreating into herself.

'Ready?' he asked as he joined them. 'Iona, will you have some supper with us?'

Perhaps with her mother there, Nya would

actually eat something, rather than just pushing the food around her plate.

'No, thank you. I'm going to go back to Penzance, but I'll be back in the morning.'

She walked partway to Theo's car with them, and then veered off to go to her own.

Once they'd picked up the food and got back to the flat, Theo got Nya settled on the couch and the fire going. Taking off her shoes, she curled up in the corner of the sofa, and closed her eyes.

Making up two trays with their fish and chips, he carried them through to the other room.

'Here you go.'

Nya sat up, taking the tray from him.

'Thank you.' Placing the tray across her lap, she stared down at the food for a moment.

'I know you don't feel like eating,' he said gently. 'But you need to keep up your strength.'

Her gaze was surprisingly fierce when she looked up at him. 'I'm getting tired of being told that.'

He shrugged, not looking away. 'Then eat, and I won't say it again, this evening.'

And, after narrowing her eyes at him, she seemed to give in, and began to eat.

They'd finished, and Theo had taken the dishes into the kitchen, when he heard Nya sigh.

'I hate to admit it, but I needed that.'

'I'm glad you had some.' She'd eaten more than he'd expected. 'Would you like a cup of tea?'

'I would, thank you.'

He turned on the kettle and put out the cups. Then, before the water could boil, his phone rang. He didn't recognise the number, but his heart started racing anyway, as he answered, 'Theo Turner.'

Nya was somehow right there beside him, by the time the person on the other end of the line spoke.

'Dr Turner, Dr Porter asked me to call and let you know that baby Hope's fever has broken, and the mucus in her lungs has started to thin. She's not out of the woods just yet, but it appears she's on the mend.'

Theo had no idea what he said—whether he thanked the caller or not—but as he hung up the phone he was aware of his hand shaking, and the sensation of his head being about to float off his neck.

'What—?'

He didn't give Nya a chance to say anything more, but punched the air. 'Yes! Hope has turned the corner.'

'Oh!' Nya sagged at the knees, and Theo instinctively caught her around the waist and pulled her into his arms.

'Our baby's going to be okay,' he said, holding her close, feeling the way she trembled.

Her face lifted to his, shining with joy, her smile making his heart sing, and Theo could no longer resist.

With a groan of surrender, he kissed her.

CHAPTER FIFTEEN

THERE WAS NO time for thought, or for doubts.

As Theo's mouth captured hers Nya wrapped her arms around him, and kissed him back.

Her heart was racing, pounding as though trying to beat its way right out of her chest, but there was no fear. Just an overwhelming sense of relief and need more powerful than she'd ever expected to feel.

She pressed closer, her entire body heating, becoming so sensitised goosebumps broke out across her back and arms.

Theo moved, his arms tightening, as he swung her around and pressed her back against the cupboard.

Now the full, hard length of his body was on hers, and Nya shuddered. Surrounded by him, she dug her fingertips into his back, wanting to make sure he couldn't, wouldn't move away.

'Nya…'

His mouth had slipped from hers, down to her throat, and she arched her head back to give him full access.

He didn't hesitate.

Nipping, licking, sucking, he searched for and found the spots that made her shiver, pulled little gasps and moans from her throat.

Desperate for the feel of his skin beneath her palms, she tugged at the back of his shirt until it came free of his trousers and plunged her hands beneath it. The sensation of goose-flesh rising beneath her fingers brought a rush of intense satisfaction.

Suddenly, Theo turned her again, and lifted her onto the counter. They were eye to eye now, and the heat in his gaze pushed her own arousal even higher. She tried to spread her thighs so he could stand between them, but her legs were tangled in her skirt, and Theo had other plans.

Holding her gaze, he pushed her cardigan off her shoulders, then down her arms, and Nya helped as best she could to get free of the garment. When his fingers grasped the hem of her blouse, his hands brushing the skin of her waist, she instinctively raised her arms.

It was off in a trice, and her bra followed immediately.

Stepping back half a pace, Theo held her hands out to the sides, and gave her now bare torso a long look, the tightness of his face telling her he liked what he was seeing.

'You're so beautiful.' Theo's voice was rough, and the sound of it brought her already tight nipples to even harder peaks.

She wanted to tell him to touch her, to do something to relieve the pleasure pressure building between her thighs, but her larynx didn't seem to want to work.

At least not until he released her hands to cup her breasts, palms supporting the weight of them, thumbs sweeping across her nipples.

Then, oh, then she cried out his name, shocked at her own reaction, already on the brink of drowning in the rising tide of ecstasy.

'Come to my bed.' It was a growl of sound. 'I want to strip you down completely. Touch you, taste you—everywhere.'

'Yes.' It didn't even occur to her to hesitate. 'Yes.'

Picking her up off the counter, he strode through the flat and down the short hallway to his room. Nya clung to his neck, peppering it with kisses, tasting his skin, inhaling the scent she'd so come to love.

Laying her on his bed, he reached over

to turn on the bedside light, his lower body not losing contact with hers. He was breathing as hard as she was, and she could feel his erection pressing against her belly. The knowledge that he was as desperate for this closeness as she was filled her with joy, and power.

Pulling him back down into her arms, she kissed him, hard, exulting when he groaned and kissed her back just as desperately.

Frantic, they rolled together, undressing each other, kissing and touching as the various bits of skin were revealed.

Then, suddenly, Theo rolled her onto her back, and trapped her there by throwing one hard thigh over her legs.

And, oh, with almost torturous slowness, he began to explore her body. Cupping her breasts, he swirled his tongue over them, nearing and then moving away from her nipples, over and over, until she stiffened and, panting with desperation, begged him to suck them.

When he complied, Nya cried out, wracked by shudders of delight.

Lost in the sensations, she twisted beneath Theo's weight, need building, rising so swiftly it threatened to overcome her, just from the blissful feeling of his mouth.

Theo slid lower, brushing his mouth across her belly, and Nya's breath caught in her chest. Shifting to the side, he used one hand to nudge her thighs apart, and Nya happily opened them to those seeking fingers.

It had been a long time since she'd felt this way, since she'd been touched so intimately, since she'd wanted culmination more than she wanted her next breath. So long that, when Theo's finger circled her clitoris, just once, she exploded into orgasm.

Her brain short-circuited. Stars danced behind her eyes. Her body shook and shook, the pleasure of it almost too much to bear.

'Nya.' Theo's forehead rested on her belly as he whispered her name. 'God, I feel as though I've been waiting for ever to touch you this way.'

It was how she felt too, but the after-effects of her orgasm made it impossible for her to do anything other than groan his name through a too-dry throat.

And Theo didn't give her a chance to recover, but slid even lower still, lifting her thighs so they draped over his shoulders. Needing to see what he was doing, Nya opened her eyes and looked down along her body to meet his dark, desire-hot gaze.

'I'm going to taste you now.' It was a statement, but he waited, as though to see if she'd object.

Her reply was to open her thighs wider in invitation, already anticipating with avid delight what that beautiful mouth would do to her equilibrium.

And Theo didn't disappoint. Instead, he took Nya to the heights of ecstasy—once, twice—until the room, the very world seemed to retreat, and it was just the two of them left.

'I want you now, Theo.' She didn't care that it sounded as though she was begging. In fact, she was. He'd brought her back to the edge of orgasm, kept her hovering there for several long moments.

She wanted to have him in every way possible.

And she didn't want to wait.

Wriggling out from beneath him, she angled her body so as to be able to swoop in for a kiss. Theo's hands were all over her, and she exulted in the way they rushed and pressed, as though wanting to explore and know every inch of her body.

Giving his shoulders a push, she got him over onto his back, and sat back on her heels to look down at him.

He was beautiful.

His body was long and sleekly muscular.

The type of frame that made all his clothes look good, but that looked even better unclothed.

And he was obviously, wonderfully aroused.

By her.

Wanting *her*.

'If you keep looking at me like that, you're going to make me lose control,' he said, in a raspy tone she'd never heard from him before, and immediately loved.

'I want you to,' she admitted, swinging her leg over his thighs. 'You've made me scream your name over and over. It's time I return the favour.'

And the way his face tightened, as she positioned herself over him, she thought there was a good chance she'd get her way.

Theo held his breath, his heart pounding, sweat breaking out on his forehead, as he watched Nya lower herself, taking him into her body.

It was the most erotic scene he'd ever beheld, and there was a part of his brain that almost refused to believe it was real.

But it must be. No dream could feel this good, could take him from aroused to desperate between one rushed breath and the next.

Nya had completely engulfed his penis, rocking her hips to take the last little bit, and it took every ounce of determination not to close his eyes. He wanted to watch her pleasure. Commit to memory the sight of Nya lost in an erotic spell they'd cast together.

She arched back, making her breasts rise, her dark, beaded nipples begging for his fingers, his lips. Putting his hands on the bed behind him for leverage, he sat up, and took first one nipple and then the other into his mouth, sucking and laving them with his tongue.

Then, as her body pulsed hard around his, he had to stop. He was already at risk of coming too soon, and he wanted this first time between them to be all for Nya.

She laughed—a breathless giggle that he thought was the most wonderful sound he'd ever heard—and said, 'Why did you stop?'

'You know why.' It was so hard to get the words out, he had to pause and catch his breath. 'You're making me crazy.'

She touched her nipples with just the tips of her fingers. 'That's my intent. To make you crazy.'

Beginning to move again, she rocked and swivelled, her breath coming faster and faster.

He was going to come, the orgasm rushing towards him with all the power of a freight train, and although Nya was obviously enjoying their coupling, she wasn't as close as he was. So, reaching up, he took one of her hands off her breast, and guided it to between her thighs.

Nya gave him a slumbrous look from beneath her lashes. 'You want me to touch myself?'

It had never occurred to him Nya would be such a frank, vocal lover, or that it would be such a turn-on.

'Yes,' he groaned. 'I need you to come for me, love. Please.'

There was no hesitation, and Theo went up on his elbow to watch as she did as he'd asked, watch her pleasure herself, her face growing tight and desperate. Hearing her cry out. Feeling her contract around him, catapulting him into his own orgasm, as she found hers.

Nya slumped over him and Theo reached up to pull her all the way down, wrapping her firmly in his arms.

She snuggled in so sweetly, and his emotions were so overwhelming just then that the words *I love you* wanted to emerge from his lips and had to be bitten back.

This encounter could just be a result of Nya's relief that Hope was going to be okay and, if that was the case, Theo refused to put her on the spot.

Or open himself up to more pain.

'Mmm…' The sound was rife with satisfaction, and hearing it reignited Theo's desire.

If this turned out to be the only time they made love—although he fervently hoped it wouldn't be—he wanted to make it memorable.

Burned into her brain for ever.

Yet, she'd hardly slept in days. Was it greedy of him to want her again, already?

To expect her to want him again too?

'Can we do that again?'

It was as though she'd read his mind. Rolling over, so they were face to face, he asked, 'Now?'

Nya grinned, reaching between them to encircle his erection.

'I was going to say, "If you're up for it," but I already know you are.'

This time as they rolled around, while the passion was as hot as it had been before, it was mixed with laughter, and that made it even more precious.

And later, as he lay with Nya in his arms, he knew he'd never felt more content, refusing to let the fear niggling at the edges of his mind spoil the moment.

Nya stirred in the night, and Theo awoke to find he was spooning her, one of her breasts nestled in his hand as though it had been made to fit there. She started to ease away, and he tightened his grip.

'I need to go to the loo,' she said, with a giggle.

'Well, hurry back.'

With another giggle, she slipped out of bed, and he watched her shadowy form cross the room.

How was it that it had taken him so long to notice how sexy Nya was?

But it was a rhetorical question. He'd been married and had trained himself not to notice things like that. Was it horrible that right now, at this very moment, he was glad Femi had left him, since that act freed him to make love with Nya?

He didn't know and didn't care. Putting the thought from his mind, he waited in the dark until he heard Nya coming and threw back the covers for her so she could dive back into the warmth of his bed. Cocooning her in his arms once more, he was considering making love to her again, when sleep claimed him.

CHAPTER SIXTEEN

NYA WOKE UP the next morning ridiculously early, with memories of the night before flooding through her, stirring her libido anew. When she took stock and realised she was alone in the bed, she rolled over to stare up at the ceiling, taking note of muscles that usually didn't ache, but were making themselves felt today.

Had it really happened? Had she really made love with Theo? Not just made love, which seemed to suggest something inherently gentle and sweet, but pretty much held him down and had her wicked way with him?

And it had been bloody brilliant.

Earth-shaking, mind-shattering, ego-boosting, orgasm city.

And utterly stupid.

Stuffing the edge of a pillow into her mouth to muffle her manic, close to hysterical laughter, Nya let herself go for a moment, trying to release the tension.

Oh, it had been magical. She hadn't even known she could feel that way—that it was possible for her to be that insatiable. But yes, it was also the last thing she should have done.

She'd been warned about the pain she would be opening herself up to. And she'd warned herself as well.

There was no future for her and Theo, and giving in to the attraction was a *great* way to hasten and intensify the future heartbreak.

So now she was left trying to figure out just how to extricate herself from a situation she actually didn't want to get out of, but darn well knew she had to.

If last night had proven anything, it was that Theo Turner's brand of loving could very well be addictive, and she couldn't afford to get hooked. Falling for a man who obviously was still grieving the end of his marriage, and who was planning an escape from the one place Nya felt safe?

Absolute foolishness.

Just the thought of it made her heart race, and had sweat breaking out on her forehead, as the remnants of her post-coital glow drained away, leaving her scared and shaky.

It would be easy to tell herself it was just the relief of hearing Hope was going to be okay that had made her susceptible to Theo's kisses, but she knew she'd be lying. The very least she could do was be honest with herself.

She'd fallen for Theo, probably from the first time she'd seen him holding Hope. Maybe, a little voice whispered in the back of her mind, from before that—when he was still a part of 'Theo and Femi'. Although she would never have allowed herself to even think of him as anything other than a friend while he was married, she'd always had a special place in her heart for him.

His quiet charm. The way he lit up a room, and made others feel important. His tenderness to and care for his patients.

And now she knew he was also a skilful and considerate lover, which just made him seem far too perfect.

Although she knew exactly how she felt about him, there was no way in hell she was letting Theo know.

Sitting up in bed, she came to a decision.

If—when—he brought it up, she'd tell him it was the joy of hearing about Hope, coupled with her exhaustion, that had created the perfect storm. That she'd reacted instinctively, and wantonly, and while she didn't regret it, it wouldn't happen again.

Couldn't happen again…

Thus determined, she swung her feet to the floor, and took a deep breath, trying to slow her heart rate.

There were no sounds from outside and as she turned on the light beside the bed she wondered where Theo was.

Obviously he'd been up for a bit before her, and her sleep had been so deep, he'd been able to come and go in the room without waking her, since her clothes, neatly folded, were on a nearby chair.

They were a reminder of the night before, and Nya blushed to see them. Then she drew herself up.

She was a grown woman, not a teenager, even if being around Theo made her feel like one.

No. If she was going to get through the next few weeks, she was going to have to brazen it out—pretend a sophistication she didn't possess. She'd put on her undies and shirt and march out of the room as though this weren't the first time in too many years to count that a man had seen her naked. As though she couldn't care less and her heart weren't about to thump its way out of her chest.

Thus buoyed, she all but flung open the bedroom door, and was instantly deflated when she realised the flat rang with the kind of echoing silence that indicated it was empty.

Well, so much for sophistication.

Wandering farther into the room, she saw a note on the kitchen island and went to read it.

Theo had gone to get them breakfast.

Nya shook her head. Why on earth did the damn man have to be so perfect?

At least she didn't have to face him just yet, and could have a shower and be properly clothed by the time he got back.

But by the time she was finished getting ready he still wasn't back, and Nya was tired of feeling as though she was on tenterhooks. Calling the hospital to check on Hope's progress took up some of the time, but not enough to calm her down.

Suddenly, she remembered she hadn't called her mother to give her the good news about Hope, and since it was now late enough to do so without waking Mum up, she put through the call.

The happiness in Mum's voice mirrored Nya's own.

'Oh, thank goodness. You and Theo must be so relieved.'

'We are,' she replied, refusing to let her

brain relive exactly where that relief had led them. 'He's gone to get us some breakfast, and then we're going to the hospital.'

Mum's sigh spoke volumes. 'He's such a good man. Seeing him with that little girl just about melts my icy heart.'

Nya couldn't help laughing. 'Really, Mum? Well, you know he's single now. Maybe—'

'Ha. Just you stop right there. I'm rather hoping he'll melt *your* heart and get you to live again.'

If only you knew...

But there was no way she'd entertain that kind of conversation with her mother.

'Mum, I told you, we're—'

'Just friends. Yes, you've mentioned that ad nauseam. That hasn't stopped me from hoping.'

'Mum, it's not like that, so don't get your hopes up. In fact, between you and me, I think Theo is planning to leave Carey Cove, so even if there was something between us—which there isn't—it wouldn't be serious, anyway.'

Mum was quiet for so long, Nya was beginning to think the conversation was over, but then a sigh came down the line.

'Nya, why does everything have to be serious? Nothing is meant to last for ever. Sometimes you just need to enjoy the moments.'

It wasn't the first time they'd had this conversation, and Nya didn't really want to have it again.

Especially not now.

'All right, Mum. I'll think about what you're saying.'

Iona sighed again. 'I doubt it, love. Kiss Hope for me and let me know when she's coming home.'

'I will.' Just then she heard Theo's key in the door, and added, 'I have to go. I'll call again later and update you, when I know what's happening.'

Hanging up, she turned to face Theo, who was putting a couple of bags down on the counter, and had to forcibly push aside the urge to cross the room to him. Hold him tight. Kiss him.

Take him back to bed.

'Good morning,' he said, smiling, although his gaze was searching her face, as though trying to decide what her reaction to him would be. 'Sorry I was so long, but it seems I was just one of a long line of people trying to get fed. The café was terribly busy.'

Time to make it plain the night before was a one-off. She made her voice brisk, as though they were discussing a patient back at Carey House. 'It's fine. I haven't been up that long anyway.'

She saw his eyes narrow, and then he turned away to open the cupboard where the plates were kept.

'Come on, then,' he said. 'Let's eat, and then get to the hospital. I just spoke to Herman Porter, and he's prepared to release Hope later this morning.'

'Oh, how wonderful!'

'Yes,' he replied, but in an absent tone, as though his thoughts were elsewhere. Then he turned to face her again, and her heart did a flip at his expression. 'Nya—'

His phone rang, interrupting whatever it was he'd planned to say, and, with an impatient sound, he picked it up and answered.

'Theo Turner. Yes. What?' He turned and walked away from her, leaving Nya staring at his back. 'Where? Yes, I'm familiar with it. Yes. We'll come as soon as possible.'

For a few moments after he hung up, he stayed where he was, staring out of the window, then he faced her, his expression inscrutable.

'That was the police. They've found Hope's mother.'

And Nya felt as though the bottom dropped out of her world all over again.

'Where is she?' she asked as she sank down onto the nearest chair.

'At Longworth Hospital, in Truro. She came in and was diagnosed with a thrombotic pulmonary embolism, and eventually admitted she'd given birth three weeks ago. We've been asked to attend at the hospital with Hope.'

'But…'

There was no way to articulate the pain sitting like a band around her chest, stealing her breath.

Theo glanced at his watch.

'How soon can you be ready?'

Nya dug deep, reaching for and finding the professionalism and strength that had seen her through everything life had thrown her way.

After all, she'd known this day would come. Later, when she was back home, she'd break down but, for now, there were things that needed to be dealt with.

She got up, keeping her back straight and her chin up.

'I'm ready now. I think, since Hope hasn't been released yet, we should go back to Carey Cove and collect her things, then come back to pick her up. At least her mum will have whatever she needs for the time being.'

'Good idea.' He nodded towards the bags he'd just brought in. 'Do you mind eating while we're driving? I'd like to get on the road as soon as possible.'

'Of course.' Forcing her trembling legs to move, she walked blindly towards the guest room. 'I'll just get my things together.'

This, then, was how it all would end. The all too brief slice of happiness she'd found was about to disappear.

Another heartbreak had found her—and she wasn't sure she knew how to get over this one.

Theo watched Nya until she disappeared down the hallway, then turned away, scrubbing a hand over his face, which had gone numb as he'd spoken to the constable.

Even though, as a doctor, he'd experienced some events others would perhaps classify as unbelievable, he'd never really believed in miracles, until last night.

Holding Nya, he'd felt as though this Christmas he was being offered something as close to miraculous as he'd ever had.

A new beginning. A second-chance family. More joy than he'd felt in years.

But even then, he'd known it was just a fantasy, and Nya's reception this morning, along with Hope's mum reappearing, showed him he'd been right to think it couldn't last.

Had it only been less than two weeks since he'd found Hope on the doorstep at Carey House? He felt as though he'd lived a lifetime since then. A glorious, wonderful lifetime, where the pain and guilt and stress he'd been living with had melted away, and he'd felt renewed.

Somewhere along the line he'd forgotten being Hope's carer was only temporary. And last night, lost in ecstasy, he'd forgotten that Nya's heart wasn't his to win—that it had already been given, lock, stock, and barrel, and there was no space left in it for him.

How ironic to finally find a path forward, after feeling so lost and stuck, only to realise it had just been a mirage.

There was nothing he could do to make any of it less painful. Wishing they could go back to a week ago, reliving the days before Hope got ill, was fruitless. It was time to face reality and face his responsibility to both Hope and Nya—which was to let them go without a fuss.

'I'm ready.'

Nya sounded so cool and in control, Theo

felt a spurt of anger, but he tamped it down. At least one of them was dealing well with the situation.

Without looking at her, he headed for the door, grabbing the bags of food and his car keys on the way.

'Let's go,' he said, knowing how terse he sounded, but unable to help it. 'It's going to be a long day.'

Long, and extremely painful.

CHAPTER SEVENTEEN

THEY MADE GOOD TIME, driving to Carey Cove and back to Falmouth to pick up Hope from St Isolde's, but to Nya it felt like an eternity, especially since the trip was a mostly silent one.

It was as though the knowledge they were giving Hope up had stripped Theo and her of all the intimacy they'd shared, and there was nothing at all left to say.

Nya felt heartsick, knowing she was losing his friendship as well. Surely it couldn't survive this latest blow.

Bad enough that she'd slept with him, but once they'd handed Hope over to Social Services and her mother, there was nothing left to bind them.

And she wouldn't try to use her love for him as a way to hold onto him. That wasn't her way. Far better to keep that to herself, rather than reveal it and make him uncomfortable.

'Why does everything have to be serious?'

Mum's question came back to her as they made the drive back to Falmouth after collecting Hope's clothes, toys, books, and other possessions.

She didn't have an answer.

For as long as she could remember, that was just how she was. The important things in life deserved to be given due consideration. Family, friends, her job. These were the things that meant the most to her, and she took them to heart.

If she didn't love Theo, then maybe she could suggest they sleep together until he left, but the reality was that if she didn't care about him, she wouldn't have slept with him at all. Even knowing he was going to desert her and Carey Cove hadn't been enough to stop her wanting him, although she wasn't one to court heartbreak.

In fact, up until this last week, she'd have classified herself as completely risk averse.

Hadn't life beaten up on her enough?

The thought made her snort.

Apparently not.

'Everything okay?'

Theo's question brought her out of her reverie.

'Yes.' Then, knowing she was being particularly terse, she added, 'Just a little sad at having to give up Hope so soon. I'd thought she'd be with us at least through Christmas.'

Theo's grunt was unintelligible, but she imagined he felt the way she did: that Christmas had completely lost its lustre.

Then she remembered that Theo's children weren't coming home for Christmas either, and sadness for him almost made her ask him to still spend the holiday with her and Mum. She quickly squelched that idea.

She wasn't strong enough to deal with that with any kind of equanimity.

The one bright spot in the day was seeing the vast improvement in Hope. Although she was still a bit congested, the infant's skin was once again pink, and her eyes were bright, rather than glazed with fever. Nya hugged her close, savouring these last moments of contact, trying not to think about them that way, but cognisant of the parting fast approaching.

Glancing up, she caught Theo looking at them, and her heart clenched. She recognised that stern distant persona. The one she'd seen fall away over the past days.

Unable to stand seeing him that way, she

walked over to where he was standing with Dr Porter and held Hope out to him.

Theo hesitated, and she thought he was going to refuse to take the infant, but Hope proved irresistible.

'Come here, my sweetheart,' he said, in that voice that never failed to melt Nya's heart. And he carried her all the way down to the car, settling her into her seat, murmuring and crooning to her the entire way.

Then they were on their way to Truro.

'I wonder what they'd do,' Theo mused, 'if we took off for the Scottish border, like a pair of brigands stealing the princess away?'

Nya shook her head, too heavy-hearted to even laugh.

'I'm not sure, but I don't think I'm cut out for life on the lam.'

'I thought you might say something like that,' was all he said in reply, before lapsing into silence once again for the rest of the drive.

Caroline Harker from Social Services was waiting for them at the hospital in Truro, and took them into a conference room when they arrived.

'Willow Carter is only sixteen,' she told them. 'When she discovered she was pregnant, she ran away from home, afraid of what her parents would say. The father was apparently a young sailor she'd met one night, and he was long gone by the time she realised about the baby. She had no prenatal medical care, and gave birth in a squat her cousin was living in. One of her friends told her about Carey House, and how kind everyone had been when her own mother gave birth there, so they got someone to drive them and left the baby there.'

'Poor little soul,' Nya said. 'What will happen now?'

'She's very confused, and frightened. We've offered her counselling and will make sure she and her baby are taken care of while she decides what she wants to do. If she ultimately decides she wants to put Hope into care, we'll make sure she gets placed in a good home.'

Nya wanted to ask how they planned to make sure that was the case, but bit the words back.

It was time to start disengaging, even though doing so was so painful she felt ill.

'I told Willow about you both, and she's asking to meet you.'

Nya looked at Theo, and they exchanged a long glance. She saw the same hesitance she felt mirrored in his eyes, but it seemed the right thing to agree.

'I'm willing,' she said, and saw Theo nod too.

Handing Hope over to the paediatric nurse tasked with taking her to the nursery felt like taking a knife to the stomach, but Nya reminded herself this wasn't the first loss she'd sustained.

And overcome.

Somehow that steadied her enough that she held back the threatening tears, but she had to turn away when Theo was saying goodbye to the infant. Seeing that would have broken her.

Nya wasn't sure what she was expecting of Hope's mother, but Willow Carter, sitting propped up in the hospital bed, looked so tiny and lost Nya couldn't help sympathising. A little slip of a girl, with big blue eyes, her complexion pallid because of her illness, she had the forlorn look of an abandoned fawn.

'I wanted to thank you,' she said, her gaze focused on where her fingers twisted in the sheets. 'Ms Harker told me you'd looked after the baby since I left her at the hospital.'

'We did,' Nya told her, reaching out to cover those restless fingers with her hand. 'She's beautiful, and so good. We called her Hope.'

Willow looked up at Nya with tears in her eyes.

'I don't know how to be a mum. I don't think I can do it. I don't want to do the wrong thing. I mean, I didn't even give her a name, before I gave her up.'

'Willow, I think you did what you thought best, and you have time to make a decision about both your future, and Hope's.' Theo's voice was soft, reassuring. 'Take Ms Harker up on her offer of counselling, and then make up your mind.'

Willow's tears were flowing, and Nya pulled some tissues out of the nearby box, and mopped at the young woman's cheeks, making soothing sounds.

'They called my mum, and she said she doesn't want to know. That if I was old enough to have a baby, I was old enough to make a life for myself.'

Nya clenched her teeth, so as not to say what she felt about a woman who'd desert her own daughter at a time like this.

The thought came to her, and before she thought it over, she said, 'Willow, if you'd like to come and spend Christmas with me and my mum, you just let Ms Harker know. We'd be happy to have you.' She gave Willow a smile. 'I'll warn you, though, that my mum celebrates Kwanzaa. Do you know what that is?'

'I do,' she said, a little spark of enthusiasm lighting her eyes. 'I read about it once. I thought that was only celebrated in America?'

'It started there, but it's spreading around the world. My mother was a professor of African studies, and that's how she learned about it. Then, the next thing I knew, we were celebrating it too.'

Nya had injected a disgruntled tone into her voice, and was pleased to see a smile tip the edges of Willow's lips.

'You'll like Mrs Ademi's mother,' Theo interjected. 'She wears the most amazing headdresses and jewellery she got from Africa.'

'She is a character,' Nya admitted. 'And when you first meet her, you'll think she's stiff and starchy, but once you get to know her, she's really very nice.'

'I… I'll think about it.' Willow didn't sound very sure, but at least now she didn't seem petrified. 'Thank you.'

'You take care of yourself and Hope,' Nya said, when they were leaving. 'And if you need anything, you tell Ms Harker to let me know, all right?'

'I will.' Willow hesitated, then said, 'Mrs Ademi, could I have a hug?'

'Of course.'

And, just like that, Nya was once more battling tears.

When they left Willow's room, as though in complete accord, they both turned towards the nursery, walking in silence to look in through the window.

The breath hitched in Nya's throat as she took one last look at the baby, who was thankfully sleeping in one of the cots. If she'd been awake and crying, Nya didn't think she'd be able to leave her.

'We should go.'

Theo's voice sounded gravelly, and Nya knew he was battling the same emotions inundating her, so she nodded, and made herself turn away, although leaving felt, oh, so wrong.

How could Nya seem so calm? Theo wondered. So collected, when he wanted to bellow at the top of his lungs, in turns angry and devastated by loss?

Of course, although she clearly loved Hope, she hadn't been building silly fantasies in her head about making a family with the three of them together, living happily ever after. No,

Nya was far too sensible for that, whereas Theo knew himself to be the consummate stupid romantic.

The kind of man who fell in love with a woman, knowing full well she would never be his.

A modern-day Cyrano, although without the overly large nose.

Caroline Harker had already left the hospital, so there was no reason to linger. As they walked through the gaily decorated corridors, Theo tried to ignore all the signs of the season. There was no joyous anticipation any more. He was hollow with grief and loss.

Once more silence filled his car as they set off back to Carey Cove, and he couldn't think of one single topic of conversation to break it.

What he wanted was to ask Nya to come home with him, to be there, so they could share their pain, and hopefully mitigate it, but he knew she'd refuse. She'd made it clear that last night had been an aberration, not to be repeated, and there was no way he'd open himself up to more agony by courting her rejection.

When they got to Carey Cove, he could see the start of preparations for the Guise Ball on the green. The Christmas tree lights were on, and a few children capered around near it, playing tag. A couple walked hand in hand along the pavement, a little boy on a scooter racing ahead of them, and he realised it was Kiara, Lucas, and Harry.

A perfect little family scene.

Seeing them made his stomach clench painfully with jealousy.

All too soon, they were at Nya's door, and she was getting out.

As he was reaching for the doorhandle, she said, 'Don't bother getting out, Theo. I can manage.' She opened the back door and took out her bags, then, before she shut the door again, said, 'Enjoy the rest of your holidays.'

Watching her walk up her front path was so agonising Theo put the car into reverse and backed out of her driveway before she'd even got inside.

Getting home, he sat in his car for a few minutes, knowing he didn't want to go inside.

For all the lights and baubles, ornaments and the tree, it would be barren, cold and lonely without Nya and Hope.

Once upon a time, this house had been home. Not always a happy one, but still the place he looked forward to going back to.

That feeling was now gone. Instead, it was like a haunted mansion, peopled not with spirits but with the ghosts of happy times and lost loves. Now he understood what Nya had meant when she'd spoken about leaving Andover after Jim died. He didn't think there would be a day when he didn't see something here that reminded him of Nya, and of Hope.

It was time to move on. Find home, or at least some kind of peace, whatever that might look like, somewhere else.

Eventually, unable to put it off any more, he got out of the car. Letting himself into the house, he went into the kitchen to turn on the kettle. While waiting for it to boil, he leaned against the cabinet, thinking about Nya.

Wishing, cravenly, that he'd met her first, before she'd known Jim. Before she'd had a chance to give the other man her heart, and then bury it with him.

Because Theo had given her his, and now he had to contemplate what it would be like to move on without it.

Without her.

CHAPTER EIGHTEEN

HER HOME HAD always been her sanctuary.
The one place where she knew she was safe,
and happy. But as she turned on the lights on
the Christmas tree, Nya knew it would never
be the same.

She'd thought Theo's utilitarian flat in Falmouth, a place where he stayed only during
emergencies at St Isolde's or if he was on call
there, had seemed sterile and lifeless. Then,
she'd thought it was because he'd made no
effort to add any personal touches, opting
strictly for function.

Yet here, surrounded by all her own personal items, pictures and art, the blankets
she'd knitted and the ornaments she'd picked
up over the years, she felt that same sense of
emptiness. All the strength she'd gathered, so
as to hold it together while they left Hope in
Truro and Theo dropped her home, drained

away, leaving her as hollow and lifeless as her cottage.

Sinking down onto the ground, she pressed the heels of her palms into her eye sockets, letting all the pain she'd been suppressing batter her in waves.

Just weeks ago, her life had seemed ideal. She had a job she loved and was proud of doing, friends she could count on, her mother near at hand. She'd been content in the knowledge that she'd been loved passionately, had loved Jim in return, and been true to that love. Living in Carey Cove, delivering babies, had given her great satisfaction. It hadn't been perfect. What life was? But it had been *enough*.

Would she ever get that contentment back? Be peaceful in spirit? Happy and grateful for all she had, without this grinding agony over what she'd lost?

What *more* she'd lost.

It overwhelmed her, hammering away at her control, and the more she fought the agony, the harder it came at her, until she was gasping with the effort to hold in her tears.

But they wouldn't be denied, and she had to, for once, let them fall, sobbing as the pain kept striking through her.

She cried for Willow, little more than a

baby herself, who'd given birth and was scared and confused. Just when she'd needed her mother, more than ever, she'd been heartbreakingly rejected.

And she cried for baby Hope, so sweet and good, whose future was uncertain.

For Theo. A man of such strength of character, such sensitivity and devotion, who'd been hurt in a way he didn't deserve.

Then for Jim, for the life they'd shared, and the one they'd never had a chance to live. For the children they'd both wanted, and the home they would have created to nurture them.

And even as she cried, she realised the truth.

Losing Jim hadn't just hurt. It had been the death of her hopes and dreams. The destruction of her future. There would be no children with Jim's gleaming, heavy-lidded eyes. No shouts of laughter over silly things that others couldn't understand. No more surprises prefaced with, 'I saw this, and thought of you.' No one who understood her sometimes better than she understood herself.

Over the years, even thinking about being with someone else had felt like a betrayal and had burdened her with guilt. It had been more comforting to lock her heart away and lean on Jim's memory. Mum had seen and tried to point it out, but Nya hadn't wanted to hear.

Besides, why love again when she already knew, all too well, that those you loved only left? Losing her father and then Jim had created an immense hole in her heart that had filled with fear.

But that hadn't stopped her from loving again, had it? Only stopped her from reaching for that love with both hands, too afraid to risk being hurt again.

Too cowardly.

The tears abated, bringing calm, and clarity.

She'd always love Jim, but he was gone, and had been for a long, long time. Because of the man he'd been—generous, full of life and laughter—he wouldn't have wanted her to lock her heart away the way she had. In fact, she thought he might be disappointed if he knew. He'd always been one to seize life and wring the most joy and pleasure out of it.

He'd have urged her to move on, to take all the love she had inside and give it away.

And Nya was almost positive he would have liked Theo, a lot.

Jim would have wanted her to take the chance to tell Theo how she felt, to risk rejection, in the hope that he would want her the way she wanted him. Loved her, the way she loved him.

She had no idea how Theo really felt about her—or whether he was ready for a relationship after his divorce. But she knew he'd touched her with tenderness and passion. And she'd seen how he looked at her when he thought she couldn't see, with the kind of longing that made her feel more feminine and sexier than she ever had before. And after all this time, without a doubt she could trust him with her friendship, trust him to tell her the truth, and, if he wanted it, trust him with her heart.

As for that last one, there was only one way to find out.

Gather her courage and tell him how she felt—without expectation. Simply because her honesty would allow them to salvage their friendship, if that was all he wanted from her.

Getting up, she went into the bathroom to wash her face, and in twenty minutes was in the car and on her way to Theo's house, her heart pounding like a bass drum.

Driving through Carey Cove, she was struck once more by how lovely the village was. With its stone and half-timbered buildings, the small, perfectly proportioned church and Georgian homes here and there, it was, in her mind, one of the most beautiful places she'd ever seen. Especially now, when everyone had taken the time to decorate for Christmas, and the village glowed with lights and festive ornaments.

Growing up here, she'd always taken it for granted. Not until she'd returned, heartsore and depressed, had she appreciated the benefits of living village life.

All the things other people complained about were the things she loved. Being instantly recognisable by name to everyone else. Having only one pub and one café, where you always knew exactly what they'd be serving. The camaraderie that brought everyone together in times of need, or simply to celebrate. Even the petty competitions that sometimes reared their heads: who made the best saffron buns, or most delicious ice cream, or had the freshest eggs.

Those, along with her work at Carey House, were the fabric and rhythm of her life.

Stopping the car near the turn-off up to the cottage hospital, where the main road dipped and went through the centre of the village, she took a moment to appreciate the picturesque scene.

It calmed her, centred her thoughts.

For the first time in her life, rather than

moving towards safety, she was stepping outside her comfort zone and embarking on an adventure. There was no way to know how Theo would respond to her admission of love, but it was something she knew she had to do for herself. Instead of her habit of planning everything, and wanting all the answers right away, all the questions she had would have to wait.

One step at a time.

And all the pain she'd been through in the past, instead of being a negative, really was the reason she knew, no matter what happened, she'd be all right.

As long as she knew Hope and Theo were safe and happy, with or without her, she'd be happy too. Or as happy as possible while pining for something you knew you could never again have.

She was stronger that she'd ever given herself credit for, and she was ready to use that strength to her advantage.

Putting the car in gear, she made her way along the lane to Theo's house, feeling a sense of homecoming that had been missing when she'd arrived at her own cottage earlier.

Taking a deep breath, she exited the car, noticing Theo hadn't turned on his Christmas lights, and wondered if that was an indication of his state of mind. In a strange way it gave her a sense of optimism, so that when she got to the front door she didn't even hesitate, but knocked straight away.

When Theo opened the door, her breath caught in her throat, and as the expression on his face morphed from polite inquiry through surprise to delight, she knew it would all work out.

Theo held out his hand and, instinctively, Nya took it, feeling as though the world had suddenly righted itself, and she was exactly where she needed to be.

Theo couldn't seem to catch his breath, anticipation wrapping itself around his chest and making him light-headed.

Nya, a little smile tipping the edges of her lush mouth, stepped easily into the house, and into his arms as the door swung shut behind her.

How could he resist her upturned lips? Why would he resist, knowing that kissing her was tantamount to being thrown into paradise?

When their lips met, and she melted against him, Theo knew that if he had his way, he'd never let her go. They fitted together perfectly—physically, emotionally, intellectually—in all the important ways.

She was what he needed to move forward and live happily again.

But he needed to know exactly why she was here.

Was it just for sex? Or something more?

Dared he actually hope that she had feelings for him that went beyond friendship with benefits?

Yet, the magic of their kisses kept him enthralled, and when Nya nudged him further into the house, he didn't resist.

She pulled back, just far enough so her breath rushed, warm and sweet, across his lips when she said, 'Make love with me.'

Everything inside him strained towards her, wanting to do what she asked without question, except the one, small part of his heart that whispered, *I need to know*.

He couldn't stand the pain, if all she wanted was the physical connection, and not the emotional.

'Why, Nya? What do you need from me?'

Nya drew back a little more, her gaze searching his, shining and intent.

'I don't need anything from you, Theo.' His heart clenched, and a cold ball formed in his stomach. 'I want your love, but that's not something to be demanded. I want your love, because I love you.'

That was all he needed to know. To hear.

A wave of heat crashed through him, washing away the icy fear. Picking her up, he carried her through to his bedroom, telling her, in between kisses, that he loved her too.

When he laid her on the bed, she twined her arms tighter around his neck, and tugged him down with her.

'I never thought I'd love again,' she whispered against his skin, before tracing the tendon along his neck with her tongue. 'You've brought me back to life.'

Later, he thought, they could talk more. Tell each other all that needed to be said. But just then he wanted to show her exactly how much he loved her, with his body, and his actions.

And it seemed she felt the same way too.

They rolled and kissed, taking off each other's clothing, touching each bit of skin as it was exposed. The scent of her filled his head, an aphrodisiac more potent than any liquor, and everywhere her hands skimmed was brought to tingling, straining life.

Time seemed irrelevant, as though they'd fallen into a place of enchantment where only they existed. Although his need grew to almost desperate levels, Theo forced himself to love Nya slowly, thoroughly. The sounds she made as she climbed towards orgasm, the way she cried out his name on culmination, pushed his own arousal even higher.

When she rolled him onto his back, and began her own slow, exploratory journey of his body, he knew it wouldn't take much for him to lose control.

As though knowing this, she teased him gently, keeping him hovering on the edge of release, then easing him back. There was something so erotic about her total concentration, he found himself having an almost out-of-body experience. As she caressed him, his vision narrowed until she was all he could see, and even though his heartbeat echoed in his ears, he also was aware of every breath she took, every soft sound she made.

Then her gaze lifted to his, and Theo reached down to pull her up and over his chest so he could kiss her, long and hard.

'Now, please, Theo.'

Her words made him tremble as though they were a touch. Rolling her to one side, he reached for a condom, going up on his knees to put it on, her eyes, dark and heavy-lidded, watching his every move.

She opened for him, her arms reaching to

hold him, pull him close, and then closer yet, her gaze not wavering, holding his captive.

And he knew that as long as he lived, he'd remember that moment as one of the most beloved of his life.

Her need for him, and his for her, were the culmination of rough roads and heartbreak, but the two of them together, just then, had created an instant of pure perfection.

'I love you,' they whispered at the same time, and Theo thought his heart would explode with sheer, unadulterated joy.

He'd planned to go slowly, give her as much pleasure as he could, for as long as he could, but Nya took control of the pace, undulating beneath him, rocking faster and faster.

Gasping, he gripped her hips, trying to return to a more leisurely pace, but she just laughed, and somehow the sound of those delicious giggles made him even wilder.

'Yes,' she cried. 'Yes, Theo. Just like that.'

Then she was coming, arms and legs locked around him, pulling him into the whirlwind of her orgasm, and he felt as though he were flying.

Still entwined, they rolled together onto their sides, lying face to face, and he gazed into Nya's eyes, savouring the present, unimpeded by the past.

Free, except for the chains of love binding him to her.

'You say I brought you back to life, Nya, but in reality you did the same for me. You and Hope filled my heart, chased away my loneliness. Made me believe in love again.'

She nodded, her smile so glorious he was almost blinded by it.

'I realised I had to put my fear aside, so as to be with you, Theo. Take the chance that you might not want me, but find out one way or another. Being with you showed me I'd rather risk everything, give up anything, if I could be with you. If you want to move from Carey Cove, and want me to, I'll go with you.'

That was when he knew, without a shadow of a doubt, that Nya loved him, fully, completely.

Carey Cove had been her refuge for years, but she was willing to give it up, to be with him.

He shook his head, then leaned in for a kiss.

'This is our home. If I have any say in it, we're not going anywhere.'

'Oh, Theo.' Throwing her arms around his neck, she hugged him hard. Then she giggled, and said, 'Maybe we should move, just so I don't have to hear my mother repeatedly saying she knew there was something between us, and telling me she told me so.'

He chuckled with her, hearing their mingled laughter like a miraculous symphony of love.

One he hoped to hear for the rest of his life.

EPILOGUE

Ever since Kiara had taken decorating to a whole new level the year before, a percentage of Carey Cove residents had been plotting to unseat her as Queen of Christmas. The result was the village being positively awash with elaborate light installations and ornaments of every style, size, and type, from old-fashioned to new wave.

'I didn't know the old village could look this good,' TJ said, as they stood in the foyer, taking off their outer wear, having just come home from a leisurely stroll down to The Dolphin for dinner. 'Nothing like a little competition to make things go completely over the top, is there?'

Nya laughed, as Theo replied, 'We almost had a fistfight the other night, at the tree-lighting ceremony, between Keith Platt and Tony Wednesday, both of whom insisted his light display was best.'

'Silly men,' Gillian interjected. 'Anyone with eyes can tell that Kiara has them beat, hands down. Right?'

The last part was addressed to Hope, who nodded, gazing up at Gillian as though the sun rose and set in the young woman.

Everything was almost perfect, Nya thought, as she headed to the kitchen to put on the kettle, while Theo and the young people moved into the living room. Life was exceptionally good.

It had been nine months since Hope had come to live with them in Carey Cove. Her mother, Willow, had tried her best, but ultimately felt the now one-year-old would be better off in permanent foster care.

But only if Nya and Theo would agree to take her.

'I want to go back to school,' Willow had told them, when they'd met to discuss the matter. 'And, to be honest, I just don't feel like I can manage her, you know? Will you take her?'

She hadn't had to ask them twice. Making Hope a permanent part of their family had felt so right.

'We'll be her surrogate grandparents,' Nya had told her. 'You'll always be her mum.'

'And always be a part of our family, too,'

Theo had added, the sentiment bringing Willow to tears.

Gillian and TJ had come to visit not long after Hope had come back to Theo and Nya's, and Hope had taken one look at Gillian and decided she'd met her idol. She'd gone crazy with excitement when she'd seen Gillian arrive to spend Christmas, and the young woman had been so sweet to Hope. It made Nya happy to see them together.

And when Mum was in the mix, it was even more adorable, since both Hope and Gillian loved being with Iona.

'There you are,' Theo said, coming into the kitchen to wrap his arms around her waist and dip in for a kiss. 'You're taking a long time.'

She laughed. 'I've been in here for two minutes. You're awfully impatient.'

'Well, it seemed longer to me.'

Turning fully into his arms, Nya raised her mouth for another kiss, then said, 'Good thing I bought you a watch for Christmas.'

'Ha-ha. You're so funny.' Theo's watch collection was already too big. Then he lowered his voice to ask, 'Have you heard from Willow?'

That was, in Nya's opinion, the one fly in the Christmas ointment—Willow's absence. True to her stated aim, the teen had gone back to school, as well as working at a store in Newquay. She called often to ask how Hope was faring, and had visited a couple of times. When Nya had suggested she come and spend whatever time off she could get over the holidays, she'd said she would let them know. She'd seemed to have enjoyed the previous Christmas spent with them, and had forged a sweet bond with Mum too, but neither Nya nor Theo had heard from her since.

'Not yet,' she replied, trying to sound upbeat. 'Just because it's already Christmas Eve doesn't mean she might not turn up.'

Dropping a kiss on the top of her head, Theo agreed.

'You're right. And your mum should be here any moment.' Giving her waist another squeeze and then relaxing his arms, he continued, 'This is turning into an amazing Christmas. The entire family here, my lovely lady on my arm. I don't know how it could get any better. Except, maybe, if you'd agree to marry me.'

Nya searched his gaze, trying to sense his mood. Last Christmas he'd told her that, as much as he loved her, he didn't feel ready to get married again, and Nya hadn't cared. She knew he loved her, and she'd promised herself that she'd never push him for anything he didn't want to give.

'Are you sure, Theo? It's completely fine for us to be going along the way we are.'

Nya had sold her cottage and moved into Theo's, and she'd never been happier. She didn't need a ring to tell her they were made for each other.

'I am sure,' he replied. 'You and Hope are my Christmas miracles, and you would make me the proudest, and happiest, man if you'd agree to be my wife.'

And what could she say to that, except a resounding, 'Yes!'?

As he pulled her close again and kissed her once more, there was the sound of a commotion in the hall. Their lips parted, but as Mum's voice and Willow's, Hope's shrieks of joy and multiple cries of welcome echoed, Nya knew, without a doubt, they'd found all they could ever desire.

Comfort.

Joy.

Home.

Love.

* * * * *